I AM CLAUDE FRANÇOIS AND YOU ARE A BATHTUB

Some Other Books by Stuart Ross

The Book of Grief and Hamburgers (ECW Press, 2022)

Sos una sola persona (trans. Thomas Downey & Sarah Moses, Socios Fundadores, 2019)

Motel of the Opposable Thumbs (Anvil Press, 2019)

Espesantes (above/ground press, 2019)

Eleven/Elleve/Alive (w/ Dag T. Straumsvåg & Hugh Thomas, shreeking violet press, 2018)

Pockets (ECW Press, 2017)

A Sparrow Came Down Resplendent (Wolsak and Wynn, 2016)

Sonnets (w/ Richard Huttel, serif of nottingham editions, 2016)

A Hamburger in a Gallery (DC Books, 2015)

Further Confessions of a Small Press Racketeer (Anvil Press, 2015)

Our Days in Vaudeville (w/ 29 collaborators, Mansfield Press, 2013)

You Exist. Details Follow. (Anvil Press, 2012)

Snowball, Dragonfly, Jew (ECW Press, 2011)

Buying Cigarettes for the Dog (Freehand Books, 2009)

Dead Cars in Managua (DC Books, 2008)

I Cut My Finger (Anvil Press, 2007)

Confessions of a Small Press Racketeer (Anvil Press, 2005)

Hey, Crumbling Balcony! Poems New & Selected (ECW Press, 2003)

Razovsky at Peace (ECW Press, 2001)

Farmer Gloomy's New Hybrid (ECW Press, 1999)

Henry Kafka & Other Stories (The Mercury Press, 1997)

The Inspiration Cha-Cha (ECW Press, 1996)

The Mud Game (w/ Gary Barwin, The Mercury Press, 1995)

The Pig Sleeps (w/ Mark Laba, Contra Mundo Books, 1993)

The Thing in Exile (w/ Steven Feldman & Mark Laba, Books by Kids, 1976)

I AM CLAUDE FRANÇOIS AND YOU ARE A BATHTUB

STORIES

STUART ROSS

anvil
PRESS

Anvil Press Publishers Inc.
P.O. Box 3008, Station Terminal
Vancouver, BC V6B 3X5
www.anvilpress.com

Cover: rayola.com
Interior design & typesetting: Stuart Ross
Author photo: Stephen Brockwell
Editor: Brian Kaufman

Library and Archives Canada Cataloguing in Publication

Title: I am Claude Francois and you are a bathtub : stories / Stuart Ross.
Names: Ross, Stuart, 1959- author.
Identifiers: Canadiana 20220242771 | ISBN 9781772141979 (softcover)
Classification: LCC PS8585.O841 I152 2022 | DDC C813/.54—dc23

Printed and bound in Canada

Represented in Canada by Publishers Group Canada
Distributed in Canada by Raincoast Books; in the U.S. by Small Press
Distribution (SPD)

The publisher gratefully acknowledges the financial assistance of the
Canada Council for the Arts, the Canada Book Fund, and the Province
of British Columbia through the B.C. Arts Council and the Book
Publishing Tax Credit.

CONTENTS

The Elements of the Short Story · 7

Regarding My Dog, Lily · 13

Ear Work · 19

Strength and Confidence · 23

Remember the Story · 27

I Am Claude François and You Are a Bathtub · 33

The Mirror Above the Sink · 37

Things Fell on Him · 41

There Were Shingles Beneath Their Backs · 45

Don't Touch People's Heads · 53

Skunk Problem at the Food Booth · 59

Hanover, 1959 · 69

Evidence · 71

The United States Has Gone Crazy · 77

The Man Who Mistook Claude François for Breathing · 81

I Am the Next Mickey Fischbaum · 91

La Papa · 95

Housing · 101

Squeak Squeak · 105

Lee Marvin, at Your Service · 113

Foot Withdrawal · 119

The "Wife" of Claude François · 127

The Burden · 131

What Is the Sound of Smoke? · 135

The Dead Frog of Love · 141

THE ELEMENTS OF THE SHORT STORY

Writing a short story is essential to creating conflict. This should happen on the first page. Begin in the middle of the action. She hits him on the head. He loses his job. The chaplain repairs the clock. Water-skiing. You have eight seconds to grab the reader's attention. Have characters. Before you begin to write, you should know everything about the setting. Where is the water fountain? Who built the piazza and in what year? Even if these facts never appear in your actual story, etc., etc.

Having been hit on the head by her, where does he fall? If you don't know this before you begin writing, you are someone who can't write this story. Do you have another job? You are not fully committed to writing the short story unless you have quit your job or unless you are unemployed to begin with. Begin at the beginning, which is in the middle of the action. Don't get bogged down in exposition. The chaplain who bent over the steering wheel of the car is wearing a hat his grandfather passed down to him who was a prisoner of war in Poland during the Second World War. The grandfather dreamed of coming to America, but, but, but—but he couldn't afford passage on the ship for his mentally handicapped younger sister, your great-aunt, so he stayed and faced his implausible doom in Eastern Europe. How did his hat then get to America? How did it wind up on the chaplain's head? Water-skiing immediately creates suspense because it is fun but dangerous.

Did I say "implausible doom" above? Do you think I meant it? No, I did not. I meant "inevitable doom." Word choice is very important in the short story. In the novel it doesn't matter so much, nor in poetry, but the short story is a compressed form and every word counts so it is good to use the exact word you meant for the exact situation. Why does he lose his job? Because he is "tired"? No, the exact word is "lazy"—he lost his job because he is "lazy." They are similar words, but one of them is different from the other and as a short-story writer, you must know these differences. She hit him over the head "deftly." The water-skier fell into the water "suddenly." He lost his job "lazily." To write well, read

8

as much as possible and circle the words you will use in your own writing.

Where is the water fountain? It is near where she hit him on the head. Is "near" precise enough? It is one block from where she hit him on the head, having been built on the piazza, which was built in 1832 during the Hapsburger Dynasty. If you have characters, you will have no problem creating conflict if they are humans because humans are naturally in conflict. Be sure it happens in the first paragraph or you risk losing your readers.

When you do read broadly (or "as much as possible"), read the greats and deep-read. If you do not know what "deep-read," a word I invented, means, look at the two words that it is comprised of and sound them out deftly. The story "Boys and Girls" by noted short story writer Alice Munroe is a perfect example. "My father was a fox farmer," it begins, and before you have even departed the first paragraph, you will find the Hudson's Bay Company, savages, calendars, forest, and a kitchen door. It is literally impossible to put the story down. Before you read on, deep-read the first sentence. Okay, now that you have deep-red it, let us examine its elements, how Munroe had no choice but to use each of those specific words to open her story "Boys and Girls" (1962). She writes "My" first. This immediately grasps the reader by the collar because even in that very first word, the writer refers to herself. If we look just a little further in the sentence, we stumble upon the word "father." "My father." This offers clues to the story setting: the story takes place in a patriarchy and likely the person who is talking the story, which we call "narrating," is a member of a nuclear family. Because she was born, her "father" was likely a heterosexual, although it never pays to make assumptions. Not long after that you zero in on the word "was." We don't even know the next word yet, but what is clear is that it is something her father no longer "is." "My father was." Mrs. Munroe could easily have stopped at these three words and have written a well-regarded story that would cinch her place in Canadian literature, but she ups the ante by following "was" with "a." A bold stroke. Why not "water-skiing"? "My father was water-skiing." A verb would have plunged us almost immediately into the action, but our writer adds the element of suspense by employing an "article," and not just any article but an "indefinite" article—the article "a." "My father was a." So not only is the reader commanded to wait a little longer to find out what the writer's father was, but once you find it out, it will not even be definite that that's what the writer's father was.

The next word in the story "Boys and Girls" is "fox." "My father was a fox." Is the story, then, not being told by a human? As we have learned earlier, it is humans who are naturally in conflict. So will this story not contain conflict? We know that it contains suspense, one of the elements of the short story, because of the fourth word, "a," which is indefinite, but now we find there will be no conflict? We simply picture the writer's father scampering through the woods. But perhaps he is looking for prey. Therein lies the conflict. If the father is a fox, then does that mean the story has been written by also a fox? Is Mrs. Munroe, who we at first assumed to be human, actually a fox?

Astute readers will be familiar with the Wild Boy of Aveyron. Also known as Victor, he lived in the woods until the age of twelve, just one year short of his bar mitzvah had he been a Jewish child, and was raised by feral wolves. "Wolf" is a common Jewish surname. Nevertheless, on January 8, 1800, just seven days after the celebration of the New Year, with all its attendant hoopla and merrymaking, Victor emerged from the woods. If you deep-read that, you will immediately realize that while Victor is a human, he was raised by wolves. Therefore it is clear that Mrs. Munroe was raised in the woods by feral foxes, including her aforementioned father.

But wait! We are not finished the first sentence of the classic story "Boys and Girls." Hidden at the very end of the first sentence is the word that is most often referred to in literary circles as the "caboose." The final word. The "clincher." When I used the word "cinch" earlier to describe how Mrs. Munroe established her place in the pantheon of Canadian literature, it's possible I might have meant "clinched." But it is not the job of the author to explain his or theirself; it is the job of the reader to interpret, given the reader's own age, sex, race, job, and life experience. The caboose, however, of Mrs. Munroe's first sentence is "farmer." Incredible! Her father was not a fox at all! He did not search for his prey in the forest! He was, in fact, a man who farmed foxes. He was a "fox farmer." Let us examine the full sentence once more.

"My father was a fox farmer."

Had Mrs. Munroe written no more than those six words, she would easily have clinched her immortal position in the annals of Canadian literature. You would be selling your self-published pamphlets of poetry on the street and she would stop to examine them. Not recognizing her, because she looked "ordinary," you would ask if she herself was a writer, because many who stop to look at your pamphlets are themselves writers. A gentle smile would spread across her ordinary "face." Yes, she would respond. Have you published? you would ask her. Yes, she would respond, her kind smile deepening slightly. What is your name—perhaps I've seen your work. And then, the clincher: "My name is Alice Munroe," she would enunciate. "My father was a fox farmer." She would then hand you a two-dollar bill in exchange for your literary pamphlet and walk down the street with it, leaving you both embarrassed and stunned, for this was no ordinary woman, but instead was Alice Munroe.

Why, you may ask, waterskiing? Because, of course, of its inherent suspense. My father was a water-skiier. My mother hit him on the head by the water fountain, a block from the piazza, which was built by the Hapsburger Empire during its reign of terror. What time did this occur? We do not know, for the chaplain had not yet repaired the clock. But one thing is for sure: the father had lost his job lazily. When the threads of a story tie up into a satisfying knot at the story's conclusion, there can be no greater frisson of satisfaction for writer nor for the reader. This is what it is all about. This is why we quit our job in order to write. This is the fox that has been farmed.

REGARDING MY DOG, LILY

I sit in the green wing chair in the northeast corner of my living room. Dust floats in the air in front of me, behind me, to either side of me. I cannot count the dust, because a) it is too plentiful, b) *dust* is a non-count noun, and c) outside it is overcast, the kind of day they call "grey," and so no sun gushes through the window to give identity to the dust. It is afternoon. Occasionally wet tires hiss by on the road outside. I sense this with my ears. There is no other sound but the occasional huff that emits from the mouth of my dog, Lily. I regard Lily from across the room. She lies on the back of the sofa. Though she calls it a chesterfield. The sofa backs up to the window, which is divided by muntins into four frames. Lily takes comfort in the cool the panes of glass give off. She takes comfort in seeing—through the sheen of grey that is this day—the grass on our small patch of lawn; the rust-coloured leaves that brush silently against the window; the tree branches that sway imperceptibly across the road; the steam that rises from just beneath the window. Lily asks me to identify the source of this steam. I tell her it has something to do with a vent, some sort of vent, possibly related to the furnace in the basement, or maybe the water heater in the basement. It is the result of something that happens in the basement, the kind of thing we do not know the mechanics of, the kind of thing we take for granted. I regard my dog, Lily. Her fur is an off-white, some honey in it, a strip of honey down her back. Aren't you cute, I say. Look how cute you are. Look at your little black-bead eyes. So intense and glistening. Look how cute you are. She stares at me but doesn't reply. Then she looks back out the window. The grey has begun to glow, just slightly. This is the sun trying to shoulder through the clouds. I close my eyes and keep them shut very tight. I squeeze them so that my face contorts, I can feel tightness around my mouth, my lips are pressed together, my cheeks strained. When I open my eyes again, everything is blurry, little blobs floating around my field of vision, my eyelashes tangled. Soon it all clears. I regard my dog, Lily, who lies on the back of the sofa, by the window. She cranes her head around toward me and lays her chin back down so that her head dangles a bit, her nose pointing at the sofa cushions. The outer fringe of her fur glows in what little sun there is beyond the window. Her body flinches, just for an instant. It's nothing to worry about. That happens to all of us sometimes. I regard my dog, and how cute she is. She has a black button nose and black beads for eyes. I can just make out her mouth beneath the off-white fur of her snout. Sometimes her ears reach up so high, but now they are flat against her head. Her body rises and falls gently. This is entitled "respiration." It is like the steam outside the window that comes from some appliance in the basement. What makes her respire is something inside of her. It is hard to believe she is so cute on the outside, but inside her she is filled with all these guts. It is as if this beautifully designed exterior is merely a vessel to carry around the inventory of her guts. When she is outside, her beautifully designed exterior, her cuteness, carries her guts from the fire hydrant to the base of a tree to a dirty patch of snow, and her button nose sniffs these things, sending signals back into her guts, which are inside her and which control her. Within her she carries organs and blood and muscles and veins and memories and anger and helplessness and mucous and microbes as plentiful as the uncountable dust in the living room. It is imperative that all these things remain inside her and that they don't spill out. Those were the exact words her veterinarian, Dr. Ruth Friedman, used when she last examined Lily. It is imperative. Lily's body swells and contracts, almost imperceptibly, as a result of the process of respiration. My chest, too, swells and contracts, as I regard Lily. I also undergo respiration. It is not something I do consciously. It is a part of nature, as much as the rust-coloured leaves that caress the window panes. Lily is licking one of her paws now. Look how cute she is. The fur on her paw becomes slick. She makes a quiet snorting sound. She stops licking her paw. She stretches her body, arches her back, settles down again. Inside me there are guts. I try not to think about them. I am a person who walks around and buys things and meets friends for coffee and inserts commas in manuscripts written by other people and picks my wife up from the airport and who misses my dead parents and yet I am little more than a sack of guts. I don't even like to think about it. Lily mentions that I have bones inside me, too. I have asked her not to remind me. I try to think of anything except these slimy organs heaving and swimming around inside me, but, in fact, that is all I think of. I am a person sitting in a wing chair, with a book on my lap, a novel whose plot I can't follow, and my body is filled with things I don't even want to picture. When I was in school, I closed my eyes when my teacher showed the film *Hemo the Magnificent*. *Hemo the Magnificent* was released on March 20, 1957, nearly two and a half years before I was born, before I came tumbling out of my mother's guts. It is in Technicolour, though I didn't see this because my eyes were closed when my teacher screened it on the screen that pulled down from the ceiling at the front of the classroom. It is directed by Frank Capra and William Hurtz. Lily points out that Frank Capra, whose middle name was Russell, also directed many films that I have watched with my eyes open, such as *Meet John Doe*. This film contains

Gary Cooper who is a onetime baseball player who doesn't know what to do with himself, and then some reporter from a newspaper says that he is the epitome of the common man. This movie was released eighteen years before I was born. Between the time the movie was released and the time I was born, there was a huge war that involved the whole world. Gary Cooper was hired to play a role in this movie, because that is what he did for a living, and yet—and yet he was filled with guts. It is hard to watch him walking around and acting in this movie without thinking about all the slimy organs suspended in all these fluids and substances inside his body. I don't know how anyone can concentrate on what is happening in that movie. I don't know how Frank Russell Capra could have concentrated on directing it. Suddenly the camera zooms in on my foot, my left foot, where I feel a tickling sensation. I look down. It is Lily's furry snout sniffing at my bare toes. She looks up at me with her black-bead eyes. A barely audible whimper emits from her, and I know this is a signal to me that she wants to go outside on the end of a leash I will hold in my hand. When Lily and I walk out the door, when we step out into the air, when our respiration involves the air outside, where it is grey, in spite of the efforts of the sun, we are the guts of the world.

EAR WORK

for Kenn Enns & for David Bouchet

I been listening to Claude François, Nick Lowe, Slothrust, the Du Droppers, Graham Parker, Bitch Stick, Screaming Females, Father John Misty. I been listening to the Swan Silvertone Singers, Bob Dylan, Jenny Lewis with the Watson Twins, Oscar Toney Jr., Car Seat Headrest. I been listening to Meredith Axelrod & Craig Ventresco. I been listening to the Clash, the Slits, the Grasping Straws, Jitensha, Captain Sensible, La Zarra. I been listening to Stockhausen and Sister Rosetta Tharpe. I been listening to Japanese

Breakfast. I been listening to Kristine Leschper, Beth Israel, Hurray for the Riff Raff, Stina Nordenstam. I been listening to the Sex Pistols. I been listening to Cannonball Statman, Ellen Foley, XTC, Adrienne Lenker, Frank Watkinson, Ben Walker. I been listening to Robert Wyatt, Sam Cooke, the Fantastic Violinaires, Joe Pernice, To the Fields, Mahalia Jackson, Randy Newman, Better Oblivion Community Center, Reina del Cid, Lucy Dacas, boygenius, Holden Main, birdheat. I been listening to the Mighty Clouds of Joy. I been listening to Zbigniew Preisner, DakhaBrakha, David Ackles, Brenda Kahn, Brian Eno, Gerry & the Pacemakers, Leon Redbone, Albin de la Simone, Alan Price, PIL, Pierre LaPointe, the Pilgrim Travelers, Van Dyke Parks. I been listening to Cathy Berberian. Today I had hoped to eat an egg-salad sandwich on pumpernickel at my favourite café and deliver decades-old newspapers to my neighbours' porches. But with a gale so brutal, I could barely open the front door. Forgive me for the pain that I have caused. I been listening to the Nutmegs, Feist, Herman Dune, Seu Jorge, Lydia Lunch, Lou Reed, X-Ray Spex, Rachel Sweet, Marilyn Moore, Kate Boothman, Frank Sinatra, the Penguins, Cub, Martin Hummingbird, Lawndale, Leo Sayer, Iannis Xenakis, Jona Lewie, Martha Wainwright, Kid Prince Moore, Mylène Farmer, Karla DeVito, Herman van Veen, Gordon Lightfoot, John Lavery, Betty Roché. I been listening to the Shaggs, Stomu Yamash'ta, Donkey Lopez, Glenda Rush, Steven Alan Feldman, Puddles Pity Party. I been listening to Los Guaraguao, Lisa Hannigan,

Camille. I been listening to Paul Quarrington, Katalena, Karl Tausig, Leonard Cohen, Phoebe Novak, Lene Lovich, Bunny & the Lakers, Matthieu Boogaerts, Weyes Blood, John Kameel Farah. I been listening to Suicide. I been listening to Emily Loizeau. Lately when I walk, I wobble. My knees point in every direction. There's no one who doesn't comment on it. Colourful cartoon birds follow me, winging circles around my head. The crimes I've committed have been morally defensible and I make no apology. I been listening to Kevin Ayers, Jane Siberry, Sister Cally Fancy, Plastic Bertrand, George Melly, Ian Dury & the Blockheads, Ted Taylor, Bobby "Blue" Bland, Warren Zevon, Talking Heads, Arthur Alexander, Johnny Cash, Kronos Quartet, Helen Humes. I been listening to Ute Lemper, Silver Jews, Michael Roth, Rachel's, Trevor Owen. I been listening to Firehose, the Jayhawks, Ida Cox, Philip Glass, Paolo Conte, Mathilde Santing, Ass Ponys, Carlene Carter, John Hiatt, Carolyn Mark, Johnny Adams, Georgie Fame & the Blue Flames. I been listening to Gavin Bryars. I been listening to Preacher Jack, the Fairfield Four, the Fabulous Poodles, Jim Moran, William Walton, Cissy Houston, Vic Chesnutt, John Cale, Nellie Lutcher, Fats Waller, Mozart. I been listening to Tom Waits and Dusty Springfield. I been listening to the Mighty Sparrow, Shelby Lynne, Scott Walker, Mo Kenney, the Huttel Brothers, Tortoise, Lambchop, the Spirit of Memphis Quartet. A man with a broken bottle is weaving toward me on the sidewalk. My teenage hero drank himself to death. My brother ignored everything the doctor told him and I have chosen a phrase from his unpublished novel to be inscribed on his headstone. I been listening to Lana Del Rey, Dieuf-Dieul de Thiès, the Barmitzvah Brothers, the Sadies, Melsie, Beth Norton, the Green Street Underground. I been listening to Sun Kil Moon, Dinah Washington, Michael Nyman, Sidney Gish, Michael Mantler, Gogol Bordello, Luis Enrique Mejía Godoy, ZGA, Adriano Celentano, Mitski, Mothers. I been listening to Sylvie Vartan. I been listening to the Four Brothers, the Five Blind Boys of Mississippi, Silvio Rodríguez, Trio, Ivor Cutler. I been listening to Hoagy Carmichael, Fire Moss, Mulligrub, Gladys Knight & the Pips, Ryan Barwin, Kevin Coyne, Rainbow Girls, the Happy Pals, Vivienne Mort. At first it seemed as if I had glided right through the glass door, as if it had been the surface of a calm lake, but then I heard the shards rain down, and my hands, my face, were covered in blood. I lay on the sidewalk and pulled my headphones back over my ears.

STRENGTH AND CONFIDENCE

There was a hubbub like you wouldn't believe. First all those people pressed against the door, and then when the door was finally opened, they poured right into the room like water gushing through a doomed ship's hull. They poured into the room and ran all over the place, looking for the piece of paper. "Where is it?" they shouted, though not in unison. As one person was saying "Where" another who had already said "Where" was saying "is" and another person who was faster than anyone else was already saying "it?" They bounced off the walls, these people, looking for the paper. "Where is it?" Then they saw that the girl actually had it, she was bent over it and writing something on it. She was probably writing her name on it. They filled up all the space around her, and their hands reached out, tentatively, drew back, reached out. They wanted the pen that she clutched. She was writing so slowly. How long was her name? Most people had two or three names, but maybe she had four or five. People from foreign places often had as many as seven names, and each of the seven names could be very long, maybe three or four syllables. Her hand froze over the piece of paper and she looked up. She saw that everyone was practically pressed right up against her, though they weren't actually touching her, and they were breathing all over her. Hands reached out and drew back, reached out and drew back. The pen was elusive. Everyone was noisily silent. "I haven't finished writing my name," she said, her voice a little shaky. Then she climbed up onto the table and peered over their heads toward the back of the room. Back there it was like a scene from a Busby Berkeley movie, but without all the girls and guys moving in unison and with no singing at all. In fact, it was just a little stage and it was empty. It was like a Busby Berkeley movie in that it was like a scene from a Busby Berkeley movie in which a radio play was being broadcast, live, and everyone was crowded around the mic, including the main characters and the guy who shook a sheet of metal to make it sound like thunder. But there were no people and no sheets of metal. There was just a mic. The people who were clustered around the girl pressed in closer.

"I am still writing my name," she said evenly. Just seeing the mic had given her strength and confidence. She climbed off the table and picked up the pen again and wrote the rest of her name, very carefully. Just her first name because they only ever introduced people by their first names. Even if you had never been there before, it was like you were their friend. The protocol was just first name. *Next up is Bob. Thank you, Bob. Next up is Pamina. Thank you, Pamina. Next up is Farouz. Thank you, Farouz. You were good in the way you said how bad pollution is.* Everybody clapped their hands because since you were finished, their turn was even sooner. The girl held out the pen when she had finished writing her first name and a hand took it from her and a body pushed up to the table until another name was going down on that sheet of paper. The girl sliced through the knot of people, and when she was free, she sat right in the back of the room, which was the front, because it was in front of the mic. She had a poem in her pocket. It was her first poem. Her friends had said it was good. More important, her teacher had said she was an asset to the class in regards to her poem. No one could believe she had never written a poem before. That's how good this poem was. In her head, she practised what she would say when she got to the mic. She would say, *God guided my hand.* She would say, *Although this poem is sad, it will offer hope if you let it into your heart.* After she read it, including the part about the boy's belly being slit open with a razor, the people would clap their hands. Then she would take out a razor for real and slice everyone in the audience's belly. There would be such a major hubbub. I'm just kidding, she wouldn't read that because she didn't write it and her poem doesn't exist and she doesn't exist. I have made her up for this, the first thing I have ever read in front of an audience. I am a person who wrote this, what you are reading now, in the book you are holding that contains also everything I wrote after this. The book is called *Strength and Confidence*. It came out six years from now. I get my ideas from everyday things, nothing special.

REMEMBER THE STORY

Remember the story about the girl who's sitting in her room and a headless chicken bursts through the door and runs around and around, bumping into walls and over-turning a floor lamp? I wrote that story.

Remember when that guy climbed to the top of a building, right up onto the roof, convinced he could fly, and then he lit a cigarette and thought for a while, and then he came walking back down the long narrow stairwell to the ground floor, convinced he was actually flying, even though he was just walking? My story. Every word.

And then the one about the guy who— He does something that involves looking up ten random people in a telephone book, and there's a woman named Maggie, and— The story is called "Ten Perfect Strangers." I don't remember anything more than that, but I wrote it, a very long time ago. It's in a box somewhere in my basement.

Amazing how I do this, how I just sit down and these ideas come flowing into my head like my head is the inside of a four-door car that has gone off the road and plunged into a small body of water, and the water begins to gush into the car, which is my head.

My friends come over to my place at all hours, and they are amazed. They see my stories lying around on the coffee table, where I just happen to sometimes leave them. Many of my friends ask me where I get all my ideas, which is a fantastic question. I bring them cold beers and pretzels, and we sit around and talk about me and my whole creative thing. Because when we were in school, none of us had a creative bone in our body. Our bodies. Somehow, though, I just got this gift. I didn't learn it. You can't *learn* it. You have to wait for it to just appear in your body one day, out of the blue, like a bolt of lightning. Also, because this gift of creativity, as I call it, is in your body, taking up room, you lose weight because you can't fit as much food inside you.

It's not that my friends don't also do remarkable things. For example, Andrew can fix a car like nobody's business. Thomas, who we call Tom or Tomboy, is in charge of distribution and promotion of a new type of embalming fluid that's better than the old kind everyone used to use. And

Pete, he can pick up a pencil, or borrow one from a waitress, and in about two minutes he can draw a picture that looks exactly like you on a serviette or a coaster. He's got a website that has everything on it.

When you are a writer, the whole world is at your door. That's what I've found. Or if not the whole world, then at least your friends. Every writer has his Andrew, Tom, and Pete. Or if it's a woman writer, her Andrea, Tamara, and Petra. (Isn't it amazing how many girls' names have an "a" at the end?) This is what we in the writing trade like to call our "audience," or our "market." It is they who consume or experience our art.

However, the life of a scribe is not one without bumps in the road, to use another metaphor. Or maybe it's the first metaphor. I can't remember if I already used one, but if I take the time to look back over what I've written, that would be time wasted when I could be getting down new words, giving my view of how the world is, the things that are important to everyone, straight from my heart. Although no young writer has ever come to me for advice, not yet anyway, if one did, one of those budding young writers, that's what I would tell them or her: if you write straight from the heart, if you are true to yourself and committed to your vision, and you include an SASE, you can't go wrong. What you wind up writing may not be everyone's cup of tea, but no one could say that you pulled the wool over their eyes.

So you are probably wondering where I *do* get my ideas for my stories. I always say you have to have "a nose for a story." You get so you can just sniff one out when you need to write something. I notice that many girls have cold noses, and I don't just mean women who I've dated. I mean any girl whose nose I've ever held, either formally or casually.

But there is an exception to this idea that girls have cold noses. Several years ago, when I was on the subway, going downtown to bring a manuscript to a publisher with whom I didn't have an appointment, I saw a lady sitting across from me. At first I thought she had just a bland, ordinary face. But when I leaned forward a bit to examine her more closely, I saw that she didn't have a nose. Not even like Betty or Veronica from *Archie* comics, who at least have a little arrow point for a nose. There was no nose on the lady's face, although there was a kind of barren plain between her eyes and her mouth where a nose might have inhabited or "set up camp."

I found myself staring at her, which is what a writer must do to gather details. Everyone else on the subway car was doing their best not to look at her, or perhaps they just hadn't noticed her. I remembered a story by a Russian writer (was it Google?) about a man whose nose falls off. He has a face and his nose falls right off it. My suspicion is that this woman just never had a nose in the first place. Wondering how she breathed without nasal apparatus, I stood up and moved closer to her, pretending to look at the ad just above her head. I saw now that she had two small perforations where her nostrils would be if she had had a nose. Therefore she had the capacity to breathe, which was a relief. To cover for the fact that I was looking at her while pretending to read the ad, I said aloud, as if to myself, "'Earn a college degree at home!' Why, I'm going to look into that." The noseless woman disembarked at the next station.

And that brings me to speak now of my own disembarkation. Because a writer must always strive for clarity, to certify that they have conveyed their meaning to you seamlessly, without the stitches showing, I don't want to overload you with my insights. My achievement here, in the time we have spent together, has been modest but not in vain. Please go about your day. I have improved you.

I AM CLAUDE FRANÇOIS AND YOU ARE A BATHTUB

You hold me in your porcelain arms and I lie in your warmth. The room is imbued with steam, and the scent of eucalyptus. I am acutely aware of my breathing. In a life that seems to move so quickly, I savour this moment. Soon I stand, a puddle of draining water caressing my feet. A light flickers on my face, and I reach up toward the lamp to tighten the bulb. If there is no light, then my beauty is invisible, and I count among my beauty the deep creases around my eyes, around the edges of my mouth, the startling squareness of my once-round chin. I become older with each year, while the women who dance onstage with me, they never age.

When my fingers touch the light fixture, there is electricity; it begins in my toes and fingertips and converges in my groin. It is like the electricity I feel between me and an audience when I am onstage singing "Cette année-là" or "Magnolias for Ever." I wear a suit of silver. The lapels of my jacket are wide. I collapse back into your arms and I am dead. I am thirty-nine.

Have I told you about my legs? They number two, and they slide comfortably into tapered black trousers. Some have said they move impossibly, they defy nature, they move in spite of me. There are two of them, the same number each time I count, and they move in two ways: At times they are abstractions, they twist and bow and slide beneath my rigid torso like rubber. Other times they are tenth-grade mathematics: their angles are precise, rudimentary, nearly mechanical. They swivel beneath me like a lazy Susan.

The women who dance onstage with me, they follow my every move: they are elongated, lanky, exquisite, wearing just enough clothing that they are not naked. They wear a treble clef or an exclamation mark. I am not certain where they come from, but they are there, onstage, exactly when I need them. What I do, the dancers do. But no, it is not hierarchical like that: we simply do *together*. In my face you can always see joy. When I sing, I *become* pure joy.

Now, at nearly forty and dead in your arms by electrocution, at the height of my comeback in a world now enchanted by disco, I am a vessel of pleasure. Just as I was at eighteen. Remember the clip for "Belles, Belles, Belles"? I threw snowballs at the women. I dressed like a Mountie. I twisted through the snow. I chose the girl. She and I locked arms. I don't remember her name now, but I remember that she was cold out there in the snow, and she was flawless.

I was born in Egypt. My mother wanted me to study the piano and the violin. But I preferred the drums, and I taught myself to play the drums. Later, when we moved to Monaco, I played the drums with an orchestra on the French Riviera. I was just a teenager. My eyes were black orbs that imparted bliss. One night I was given the opportunity to sing, and though I had never studied singing, the audience liked what they heard, my unpractised voice, its deep timbre. Encouraged by this success, I went to Paris to make my fortune. I climbed into you nearly two decades later, into your curved and welcoming arms, your intoxicating warmth.

The derivation of the Americanism *electrocution* lies in the words *electricity* and *execution*, and the French adds only an endearing cowlick to the first vowel with *électrocution*. It originally meant the intentional death of a condemned criminal but later came to include any type of death induced by electric shock, such as the accidental death of a beloved pop singer in his Paris apartment on March 11, 1978, as he bathed, hoping to relax the day before the taping of a television appearance. I had avoided death so many times before. I fell, I stood, I fell, I stood, I fell, I stood, always accompanied by my beautiful dancers. In 1971 I collapsed from exhaustion during a performance. In 1975 I was nearly obliterated by an IRA bomb. In 1977 a fan tried to end my life through the barrel of a gun, a traditional expression of love I cannot understand.

I will never be onstage again. I will never again sing pop or rock 'n' roll or disco. The camera will never capture the tenderness in my features as I sing a ballad. I fear for the girls, girls, girls, and the grief they will feel at my death as the streets of Paris overflow with mourners. I never wished to evoke grief: never. Even when I sang a sad song, a song like "Ça pleure aussi un homme," I strove to convey a beauty that would conquer the sadness. I am blond, and my eyes are dark, though they sparkle playfully. My smile is my best feature. See my legs go.

I have learned that phrasing is everything. It is the key to ensuring that what you utter in song carries the meaning you intend when it reaches the listener's ears. One longs to embrace just a single sentence that could be received by one's fans with precision of intention, with sacred purity. Would this were possible, for me that sentence would be this: *I existed for joy.*

Beloved bathtub, you cradle me and I am still and the water has drained, only a few droplets still cling to my body, my immaculate face. My left cheek presses against your cool, smooth belly. The steam has dissipated. In the next room, a gold-lamé suit is laid out on the bed.

I dream myself into that suit.

I make my legs move.

THE MIRROR ABOVE THE SINK

She wakes earlier than me, with the alarm. I'm not ashamed, because I stay up later than her, hours later. When I come to bed, I hear the plows shovelling snow off the streets and sometimes the newspaper hitting the front door. I lay my head on the pillow and listen to her steady breathing, her luxury of sleep, and then soon I am asleep. Or sometimes an hour later I am asleep, finally asleep. I dream something terrible, if I even remember my dream. I dream that storm troopers are chasing me through the halls of the school, or that storm troopers are banging the butts of their rifles against my front door and it's beginning to splinter. And soon I am awake, just barely, and I reach over for her but I feel only mattress. She is awake. I hadn't even heard the alarm. I drag myself out from under the covers and shuffle out of the room, naked and heavy-lidded. I am trying to remember how many hours of sleep I have gotten— three? four?—as I head down the hall toward the bathroom. I pass the door to the living room, and the light is on there, and she is lying on the sofa, her knees drawn up, a book propped up against her thighs. She is writing. The book is her journal. It is still dark outside at this early hour, and she writes by the light of a small lamp behind her. She looks up at me and smiles and says go back to bed it's early, and I force a slight smile and continue on toward the washroom. What is she writing? I wonder. Why does she need to write so early in the morning? To write when I'm asleep? Was her smile real? She always smiles at me like that. It must be easy for her, like turning on a tap. I shut the bathroom door and look at myself in the mirror above the sink. I turn on a tap. It looks like someone has taken a chunk of coal and rubbed it roughly under my eyes. I try to remember when it was I last shaved. I wonder if I will shave today or if I will try to get away with another day of not shaving. My father shaved every day. He was committed to shaving. The hairs on my chest are all white. I remember how old I am. I am old but not old enough to have a chest of white hair. Is that what she is writing about? How disappointing it is that my chest hair is white? Or that I do not shave every day? That I do not care enough about her to shave every day? Why else would she wake so early to write in her journal? Clearly she feels trapped with me. She wants to get out of this house. To start a new life somewhere else. She crosses that out. No: she wants to get *me* out of the house. She wants to start a new life right here, with me gone, every trace of me. But she knows I will be lost without her. I will carry my small bag of belongings down this street, and turn onto that street, and turn again, and again, then find myself on a street I don't recognize. Then I will fall into a ravine and hurt myself. I won't be able to get up. Seasons will pass. Hedgehogs and raccoons will nibble at my body. They like how my unshaved cheeks and chin feel against their dense fur. She is writing about the derivation of the word *hedgehog*, how it came into the English language in 1450, the year of the birth of Hiawatha, and of Hieronymous Bosch. She writes of Bosch's surreal nightmarescapes. With me gone, with the clarity my absence will bring, she can wake from the nightmare of the past decade. She remembers tenderly—she scratches that out and puts *almost fondly* instead— our first few dates and how I made her laugh, how I brought her unusual gifts that set me apart from the other boys who attempted to charm her, the more handsome boys, the more athletic boys, the more obvious boys. She liked me because I was unusual. I wasn't like the boys she was used to: those who would have successful careers and never, in throes of angst, question the reason for their own existences. But it didn't take long for the novelty to evaporate. Unfortunately we had already moved in together. She corrects this to *he had already moved into my place.* I run a toothbrush quickly across my

39

teeth so that the tap water will not be wasted and I spit into the sink, and then I flush the toilet so she doesn't suspect that I've been standing in the washroom for the past five minutes staring at my swollen, unshaven face in the mirror above the sink. I place a hand on the doorknob and I'm about to turn it when I hear the deafening scratch of her pen against the page of her journal. *He places a hand on the doorknob,* she writes. *Soon he will open it and he will come into this room, tentatively, and when he looks at my face, he will know it's all over. He will pack a small bag of his belongings and, without a word, he'll walk out the front door, into the cold morning.*

THINGS FELL ON HIM

Things fell on him, things from trees, from eaves-troughs, from the windows of apartments, from passing airplanes. Space junk fell on him. Monkeys in astronaut suits. Acorns and dead leaves, whirlybirds and pine cones. Sap, and also the rancid droppings of condors. Hub caps fell on him. Toothbrushes. Piano benches. A rare Hank Snow album.

People watched from across the street. They pointed and laughed. He crossed his arms above his head protectively and crouched on the sidewalk. Men and women walked by on both sides of him, gripping shopping bags and briefcases and children, but nothing fell on *them*. It was like they were somehow special, he thought. Everyone in the world was special except for him.

Thing is, it cost the city an awful lot to clean up after him. Some conservative members of the city council thought maybe they could make him financially responsible for the destruction that followed him everywhere he went, but the more progressive caucus pointed out that it wasn't his fault. He didn't actually *do* anything to make things fall on him. At least, not so far as anyone knew.

His was a life of bruises and scrapes and concussions. Spilled grocery bags and torn jackets, like in the place where the sleeve attaches to the shoulder. Don't get me wrong: it wasn't like things fell on him every day. Sometimes he'd have a two- or three-day streak in which there were no falling incidents. He found, though, that he couldn't relax. He had to be constantly vigilant. His heart pounded at the slightest sound from above. When he walked, he took each step like he was testing the temperature of lake water with his toe.

Okay. A guy from the newspaper interviewed him. They were sitting in a café. Halfway through the interview, a stuffed moose head tumbled from the wall, and its antlers scraped his scalp. "I remember when I was but a baby," he was saying. "I lay in my crib and I thrashed about with my tiny arms and legs and I stared up at a beautiful mobile my parents had hung above me. It had animals and vehicles and flowers, in all the splendid colours that plastic comes in. My parents were very particular about the lighting in my room—it was always as if I were under the shadow of a weeping willow on a sunny day—and the giraffes and dump trucks and daffodils twinkled gently above me."

The guy from the newspaper asked, "Did it fall on you? The mobile? Did this whole thing start happening when you were a baby?"

"It was the best time of my life," the man said, holding a bloodied serviette to his head. "My dreams brought me comfort, and when I was awake I could soar up into the mobile and play with purple armadillos and zoom around in a green Camaro and sniff the red geraniums. A breeze wafted in through the window and all the hanging components of the mobile danced gaily around me. I have never again been so happy as I was in those early months, long before I realized I was a person who wasn't special in any way."

After this interview appeared in the newspaper, alongside a photograph of his kind but anxious face, he received dozens of marriage proposals from across the country. He sat in his kitchen and read them, spreading the enclosed photos on his table, as chunks of plaster fell on him from the ceiling and the light fixture overhead trembled.

One letter came from a woman named Paloma who lived in Yellowknife:

> Come with me. Together, we will soar higher than anything else. Our ascent will be limitless. Nothing will be above us, and so nothing will fall on you.

She had drawn a picture of a stick man and a stick woman holding hands, with rays emanating from their featureless round heads.

He brushed the plaster dust off his thin forearms and sat back in his chair. He thought about the top edge of the universe. About that glorious moment when his head, then his shoulders, then his torso, would burst through and nothing—absolutely nothing—would be higher than him.

He stood up and walked across the kitchen, peering up through the small window above the sink. The journey would take a tremendous toll on his body, a terrible toll, but it would be worth it. It'd likely be months before he could walk around feeling relaxed, before the jitters subsided, the constant sense of foreboding. Before the bruises faded and the throbbing in his head and in his gut subsided. But then there would be calm, the serenity he had always dreamed of.

In the morning, he quit his job, gave away his possessions, unscrewed the mezuzah from his door frame, put on some comfortable but warm clothes, and set off for the top of the universe. As he passed a small flower stand near the bus stop, he dug into his pocket for a few coins and bought a single red geranium for Paloma.

THERE WERE SHINGLES BENEATH THEIR BACKS

Howie was lying on the roof of the house in some damn neighbourhood he knew he'd been in before, but he couldn't recall when he'd been there or where he was. Mr. Cage lay beside him, his breathing shallow. They both felt the same breeze lick at their necks and foreheads. When they opened their eyes, they looked at the same clouds blotting out the same stars, and recognized the occasional pterodactyl winging by, its black silhouette just visible against the slightly less black of the clouds.

"Has it come to this?" Howie said quietly.

Mr. Cage let his eyes fall shut, having had his fill of the clouds.

"In what way are we related?" Howie asked.

A short explosion in the distance. A car backfiring, a gunshot, a brick hitting the pavement.

Mr. Cage cleared his throat. He could just barely speak through his cancer now. It made his clothes fit better but it made it hard to speak. He stuck out his tongue to find some cool air. He had something to say and needed to cool his throat.

A drop of rain fell. It landed on his tongue.

Howie opened his mouth and stuck out his own tongue. He got a drop, too. They had been friends for so many years, but Howie couldn't remember how they'd met. There was a desert and there was a car. Some women playing mah-jong. Six strips of kosher beef fry in a Teflon pan. A TV tuned to the moon landing, the vertical hold unstuck.

"It's incumbent..." Mr. Cage coughed. A breeze cooled his face. "It's incumbent upon me to tell a story, Howie, at this particular time in my life. Here on the roof. Cells dividing within me, out of control."

Howie cracked his knuckles.

"On the last day I saw her," said Mr. Cage, "the day before she was to fly to Albuquerque, or Vienna, or the moon, or Kosovo, or wherever she was going to study, I don't recall precisely the location now, I touched her hand, I held it, I kissed it once or twice. I caressed her shoulder, which was bare, it was a very hot day. I put—" Mr. Cage coughed, then rested for nearly a minute. What was happening to him?

Howie reached up, like he could plunge his fingers through the clouds and clutch one of the stars behind them and light his cigarette with it. But his fingers didn't even come close to the clouds. "Perspective," he said. "It's so weird."

"As we walked," said Mr. Cage, "I put my arm around her. My hand rested on her upper arm. As we sat on the beach, I touched the toes that poked out from the end of the sandal she wore on her right foot. I took her right cheek lightly in my left hand, and my hand remained there for maybe six seconds, and, Howie, she gazed at me with an expression I couldn't read."

Mr. Cage rested again. He wished he had a nectarine.

Howie thought of his Grade 2 teacher, and her sandals. She walked around in front of the class wearing sandals. Howie remembered this distinctly from when he was seven years old. His father, on Meet the Teachers Day, said afterward to Howie, "Your teacher, she's a real knockout." Howie thought he was saying she was a boxer. There were straps going up from her sandals almost to her knees.

Mr. Cage felt his body start to melt, even though the air was cooling now. "I touched her arm briefly, as I made conversational points, too many times to count, Howie, and when we parted, I brushed my lips against her cheek, just a single light kiss that might have felt like a fly landing on her cheek and then immediately taking off again, that's how light and brief my kiss was, Howie. You going to arrest me? I plead guilty before the jury of my peers."

Howie was imagining his Grade 2 teacher in a boxing ring. He got close enough to smell her sweat, and then she delivered a right jab that sent him to the mat. It was the best day of his life. Everyone in the crowd was smoking cigars and cawing at him, cash registers were ringing, his lips were quivering, a siren wailed somewhere out in the streets. He opened his swollen eyes and gazed at his teacher's ankles.

"The next day, she was rushing to the airport in a rented car, Howie. Avis, Budget, Ventricle—one of those places where they rent you a car. I sat on a bench staring into the lake. There were clouds in the lake. That's the way it looked. Those were the clouds into which she would soon soar. The bench was hard against my skinny ass, Howie. I thought about her and about all that touch I had initiated. You see, she had initiated none." Mr. Cage thought about the word *initiated*. Had he ever said it aloud before? Was that among the words he had used when he was alive? It seemed unfamiliar.

At once, Howie was conscious of the shingles against his back. He thought about the word *shingles*. When he was a child his parents told him his grandmother, Ruth—was her name Ruth?—had shingles and he pictured that if you took off her floral-patterned shirt and looked at her from the back you would see roofing shingles running downward, green shingles, from the base of her neck to her lower back. Had his parents taken off her shirt? That didn't seem like a thing that would happen, so maybe he was inventing this memory.

"Howie. There was this one time, once, as we stood on a ferry, moving in slow motion to an island where we'd chosen to spend a few hours, when she briefly laid her head on my shoulder. Was it an act of comfort, affection, perhaps one of exhaustion? I ran this moment through my head again and again, Howie, but I could not arrive at a definitive answer. Meanwhile, her plane was lifting into the air, and I didn't understand how this was possible: both that she was leaving, she would soon be gone, and that a huge mass of metal could rise from the ground and keep rising, filled with people and suitcases and food. They have—"

Mr. Cage's body rattled. Howie felt the vibrations beneath him.

"They have kosher food on the plane, or if you're a Muslim they have Muslim food. I kid you not, Howie." Mr. Cage reached a hand out toward Howie. They had never held hands. That would be crazy, two men. Back in the days when Mr. Cage was a young man, it would be a police thing. "I wondered if my touch—what was likely my excessive touch, a quantity of touch that far exceeded the total amount of touch I had initiated over the entire goddamn previous decade put together—whether that touch caused her sadness, whether it was something she simply tolerated, whether she wanted to reciprocate but could not, for whatever reason, whether she would wear an asbestos suit should we ever see each other again."

Howie dug his fingers into the shingles. He didn't want to fall off the roof.

"On that final day we were together, Howie, I touched her perhaps twenty-four per cent of the times I wanted to, whereas on all the days we had spent together before, in those precious years when she held her feet to the ground in the city in which I lived, I touched her, on average, only two per cent of the times I wanted to. And this does not include the one hundred per cent of the time I wanted to lightly press my lips to hers, hoping perhaps she would press hers back against mine. I stayed awake at night, composing in my mind a letter to her in which I asked if she might kiss me on my deathbed, just once, presuming I was able to let her know I was on my deathbed, though it was equally likely I would die sitting in a chair reading, perhaps reading a Hardy Boys book, *The Mystery of the Fucking Whatever*, since my intellectual capabilities would have so steeply declined.

"Would she kiss me on my deathbed, Howie? In my deathchair at the kitchen table as a fork dropped from my hand? In my deathcar as I slammed into a tree? I should add that she would be thrown out the window to safety."

Howie pictured his Grade 2 teacher looking at herself in the mirror. "Not a scratch," she would say, turning this way and that. Howie realized he could no longer feel his grandmother's shingles digging into his back. In fact, he felt cool air on his back, cool air beneath him. Was he actually floating in the air? It had been a long time since he had floated in the air.

"But I knew that didn't matter, Howie. Here is what mattered: that the contact of my finger or hand or lips against her shoulder or hair or cheek or toes or arm or hand or fingers did not cause her any distress." Mr. Cage became aware of his hand. It was empty. It had set out to find Howie's hand, but it was empty. How long had he and Howie known each other? Had one of them helped the other hide a body? Who had slept on whose sofa? Who had apologized to whom?

Howie was sinking into the ocean. Bubbles floated up from his nostrils. "When her plane lands," he murmured, "the earth will heal and the oceans will become pure again and the storms shall subside, and she will reach out her perfect hand, each of its five exquisite fingers rippling in the breeze, she will reach that perfect hand into the future and the future will take that hand and pull her tenderly into itself."

Mr. Cage pressed his eyes shut. When he was a kid and he did this, pressed his eyes shut like this, he'd see blobs floating around, undulating coloured blobs drifting over the veins of his eyes.

But that was the past and this was the present.

Did they occur at the same time?

Did everything happen at once?

Mr. Cage felt things taking place inside him that he had never felt before. It seemed a distant memory now, but had he actually held his hand over another man's face until the other man stopped breathing?

"Howie, teach me to swim," he said.

DON'T TOUCH PEOPLE'S HEADS

A woman was kneeling by the bottom shelves, looking at the wide variety of cheese slicers. The one she admired most was like a small guillotine. She lifted up the blade and let it fall several times. She imagined an aged cheddar, some havarti, a nice brick of Danbo. And then she felt something in her hair. Her hand automatically whipped up and brushed it away.

"Don't touch people's heads!" she heard from behind her in a man's deep voice.

"It's just a head on a lady's shoulders," said the voice of a child, a little girl.

The woman stood up, which was way more difficult than it had been a few years earlier. Her knees were speckled with stabs of pain. She turned around and saw a man in a thick sweater—one of those sweaters with a moose, a lake, some trees—walking away down the aisle, his hand grasping a child's tiny hand, the child's feet dragging along the floor.

"Get up and walk!" said the man to the child.

"It was just a head!"

The woman reached up slowly and ran her fingers through her long, dry hair. It had felt like a bug, that feeling in her hair, or a fluttering cobweb, but it was only the girl's hand that had touched her head.

Don't touch people's heads, the father had said. The father had actually *admonished* the child. Who admonished kids these days? What happened to respect for children, for the rights of children on a planet that was going to be handed to them on the brink of disaster?

The woman stood there in the aisle of the kitchen store and let her eyelids fall shut. She slowed her breathing and remembered the child's touch. Gentle as a cobweb. She felt the child stroking her hair, stroking her head, murmuring, *There, there,* in a quiet voice. She felt the cancer inside her slowly evaporate. The diseased cells shrinking until they had vanished. Her organs felt light and robust. The woman could picture her kidneys and her liver and her pancreas drifting through a blue sky, bursting in slow motion through cottony clouds. Her organs were sleek and healthy and glistening.

She saw them float beyond the clouds and over a lake. They joined other organs that seemed to suddenly appear, like stars twinkling into existence. Together they disappeared over the calm, watery horizon.

"A flock of beautiful, healthy organs," the woman said aloud.

For the drive home, she took the road that ran alongside the river, past all those little bungalows that looked almost like cottages. It meant an extra ten minutes behind the wheel, but she didn't much care about time. The fingertips of her right hand played with the radio dial. She didn't stay on any one station for more than thirty seconds. She was looking for exactly the right song, but she couldn't have even said what it was. For the first time in several months, she felt at peace. She tilted the rear-view mirror toward herself and stole a quick glance at her own eyes, just to confirm that she was herself, then adjusted the mirror again so she could see the road behind her.

The woman liked the feeling of not having organs inside her body. It gave her a certain lightness. It gave her less to worry about. This way, without the burden of organs, there was less to go wrong.

At home, she put away the box with her new cheese slicer and plugged in the kettle. The doorbell rang, then someone knocked twice. As the woman walked toward the front hall, she passed some framed photos on a telephone table and paused. A young man in a black graduation robe. A girl on a pony. The girl, grown up, holding a baby and smiling into the camera. A man and a woman leaning against a station wagon parked on a country road. She said, aloud, their names, all their names, the name of the young man, the girl, the baby, the couple, and she tasted peppermint in her mouth.

When she opened the door, a small girl stood on her porch. It was the girl from the house across the road. Her hair was brown and long. She wore blue jeans and a pink T-shirt with a sparkly gold fox on it.

"Can I play with your spinning wheel?" the girl asked.

The woman opened the door wider, and the girl ran into the house and up the stairs to the studio above the garage. The woman went to the kitchen, poured a glass of ginger ale, put a red-and-white-striped straw in it, and followed the child up. She stood in the doorway, watching the girl spin the slender wooden wheel. The wheel was like the ripples in a pond after a baby frog jumps in. The girl's hair hung down her back, nearly to her waist.

The woman came to stand behind the girl and set the glass of ginger ale on a small table. Slowly she raised one of her hands and placed it on the child's head, barely touching, and felt the silky brown hair against her palm.

"It's fast!" the girl said, leaning back from the spinning wheel so she didn't lose any fingers.

The woman's hand rested lightly on the child's head. It would take a scientist with incredibly sensitive instruments to determine the exact space between palm and skull, but there was no scientist present, no scientist in this house.

The woman closed her eyes and felt the warmth that flowed up into her from the child. She remembered when she was a child herself, when she bit both ends off a piece of licorice and drank Coke out of a bottle with it, when she played with her grandmother's spotted dachshund, when she watched her mother fry up a pan of macaroni and cheese, when she borrowed Petunia the Goose books from the library and read them perched in the branches of a tree.

Her eyes still closed, she smiled. She listened to the girl sip the ginger ale through the striped straw. The ginger ale went into the girl's body.

Eventually, the woman's organs descended from the feathery clouds and alighted on a beach covered in white sand. There were organs everywhere, glistening nearby and in the distance. When the woman's organs had oriented themselves, they headed for the shade of some myrtle trees up the beach and made themselves comfortable. The cool breeze caressed them.

Imagine you were a hermit crab burrowing on that beach. Okay, so you're digging and digging, and then this one time, you pop up out of your hole and you see all these organs on the beach. Organs draped all over the white sand.

Where did they come from?

How did they get here?

It's the weirdest thing you've ever seen, and you've got eyes that extend from your head.

SKUNK PROBLEM AT THE FOOD BOOTH

Solly knocked his head on a low-hanging birch branch as he ran toward the crowd that had gathered at the food concession. He hit the ground hard, lay unconscious for three days, and when he woke, the Pioneer Village was deserted. Not a visitor or staff member in sight. His stomach churned and he felt nauseous. He wondered what had happened to his wife and to Sim. Had they really left without him? Or were they wandering the empty village right now, looking for him in the old church, the red schoolhouse, the office of the *Village Tribune*, the Cheese Factory, the Town Hall?

The Pioneer Village was situated in a rural stretch of gently rolling hills, several kilometres from a major highway. So there were no car sounds—no engines, horns, brakes, or collisions. Solly heard only the rustling of breeze-agitated trees. The mechanical buzzing of a cicada. The groan of his stomach demanding food or demanding to puke.

Three days had passed, but Solly didn't know three days had passed, only that it'd been a long time, because he'd never felt so hungry. Now he remembered the crowd, the commotion. They had been gathered around the food booth. There'd been some kind of hubbub there. He swivelled around and saw, beyond a cluster of pine trees, the small wooden structure. It said HAMBURGERS on it. It said HOT DOGS and POTATO CHIPS. COLD DRINKS. ICE CREAM.

Solly started walking along the dirt path that threaded through the village, connecting all the buildings from a century past, a century and a half. He passed a large flatbed wagon parked in the path. It was heaped with hay. Now he remembered: he'd sent Carla and Sim on a hayride so he could sneak off and have a smoke. He remembered waving to them as they sat on the back of the wagon, pulled by a pair of old grey horses. Solly wondered where they kept the horses when the Pioneer Village was closed. Maybe they didn't keep them on-site. Maybe some local farmer brought them in on loan for all the various events: for Pumpkinfest, Hay Daze, Haunted Tour, Shear & Cheer.

Solly felt a chill and became aware how soggy his clothes were. It was early morning. The grass, which he had been lying in, was glistening with dew. Dew sparkled on spiderwebs dangling from trees. He heard now the crow of a rooster. The hum of—what was the creek called?—the hum of Carpenter Creek.

The food booth was still open. Not open for business, just unlocked. Solly saw a paper plate of wizened French fries, streaked with ketchup and crawling with flies. It sat on the serving counter, having never been picked up. He pushed through the small half-door that swung in toward the kitchen space. Deep fryer. Fridge. Cutting board. Shelves of buns. Solly grabbed a bag of hamburger buns off a shelf and ripped it open. He squirted some ketchup on a bun and took a few bites. His teeth and tongue needed convincing. He forced them to follow through with their task.

Outside, there were half a dozen picnic benches, one of them strewn with empty pop cans. Some of the cans stood up, some lay on their sides, rocking incrementally in the breeze. Solly sat down at one of the tables and crossed his arms on the wooden surface. He closed his eyes gently and tried to piece it all together.

The Pioneer Village had been built, Solly remembered, in a place where there had not been a Pioneer Village. There was, however, a grist mill, a beautiful stone grist mill, and that was why the village was put here. All the buildings were moved in from around the broader region and set up to create a little village. By any standards, by the standards of any century, it was an unusual village. A village with one of everything.

A model village made up of buildings moved from villages built where other people had been displaced: displaced from their rice beds, their trading routes, their hunting grounds.

Solly recalled that after the wagon carrying his wife and son had disappeared down the path, he had wandered off behind the Old McGregor House to light up a Lucky Seven. While he was drawing the smoke slowly into his lungs, he'd heard laughter from inside the two-storey structure. He took a few steps toward the window and peered in. A woman stood by the fireplace, and in the fireplace hung a large cast-iron pot. The woman stirred its contents with a long tin ladle, and he recognized her. The woman was Evie Hyman. She wore pioneer garb: a big blue dress, white apron, ruffled sleeves, a bonnet.

Back in high school, Solly had asked Evie Finkelstein, as she was called then, to go on a date with him. There was a stage adaptation of the *Archie* comics being presented at the East Side Secondary School, on the other side of town. Evie had smiled a real genuine smile. But she was already going to the play with Beanie Hyman. Maybe she and Solly could do something else sometime. Even though she'd been totally gracious, Solly felt embarrassed, and soon they graduated, and Solly went to Montreal to study engineering, and at some point, he heard that Evie and Beanie had gotten married, become orthodox, and were raising four children.

Now here she was, stirring up dandelion tea at the Pioneer Village and ladling it into little paper cups for the visitors to taste. Had she really traded in the name Finkelstein for Hyman? That's what Solly found hard to believe. It was a lose-lose proposition.

After a few moments, Evie had stood up straight and turned toward the door, her back to Solly. She lay the ladle down on a wooden stool and ran from the Old McGregor House. Solly wondered if she had dreams of being Evie McGregor, but he didn't wonder long, as he became aware of a commotion in the distance.

That was when he'd started running, too, and the last thing he remembered was all the running. Boys in suspenders running. Women in hoop skirts. Bearded men in straight black pants and elbow-patched jackets. Some of them carried farm implements. Some laughed, some shouted.

That was three days ago. Now Solly ground the last of the hamburger bun between his teeth and forced himself to swallow the dry mass. Opening his eyes again, he was surprised by how bright the sun was. He swung himself off the bench and walked back to the tiny kitchen. The cupboards were all open, food and supplies scattered on the wood floor. Why hadn't he noticed this before? And an axe—an axe had been slammed into the food-prep counter.

He grabbed another hamburger bun off one of the shelves, stuffed it into his pocket for later, and set out along the path that led to the entrance of the Pioneer Village. Alerted by a metallic clanging, Solly swung around to look at the blacksmith's workshop. Was someone in there making horseshoes or something? But then he saw a padlock swinging against the metal plate that housed the door handle. His heart slowed down again.

Passing the Old McGregor House, he glanced through the open front door. The large front room on the ground floor was empty. The black pot, presumably filled with cold dandelion tea, hung motionless in a cold fireplace.

Soon Solly was stepping through the back doors of the General Store, which also served as the village's Ticket Office. The shelves were sparsely stocked and tidy. Jars of maple syrup. Small boxes of chocolates in the shape of maple leaves. A Pioneer Puzzle: 312 Interlocking Pieces That Paint a Rural Scene Worth Framing. Key rings with little horseshoes attached, and nameplates in moulded plastic made to look—just barely—like wood. A package of perforated cardboard sheets that, assembled, create An Authentic Steam Engine Just Like Our Great-Grandfathers Operated!

Solly's great-grandfathers had lived in Poland. One was a ragman and the other a tailor. Solly had been named after the ragman, Simcha, his mother's grandfather. These guys had big grey beards and thick eyebrows and dark eyes and they wore black clothes. They spoke Polish and Yiddish. He imagined they ate kreplach and thin soups and chopped liver. Solly had no idea what his great-grandfathers did for fun, or even if there was such a thing as fun back then.

Solly passed by the admission counter, drawing his fingertips lightly along its surface. A large jar on it contained small bits of folded paper. Raffle tickets. He remembered buying a raffle ticket when he came in. The prize was a hideous quilt. He had hoped he wouldn't win.

He stepped out the front door of the General Store and gazed past a quartet of outhouses and a rudimentary gazebo. A grass field stretched far back to the country road that meandered about seven kilometres farther to the highway. The grass field was covered in cars, parked in long neat rows. All those cars. No people. Suddenly dizzy, Solly reached out to steady himself and found his hand grasping an easel with a chalkboard perched on it.

In ornamental red hand-lettering, it read:

WELCOME TO PIONEER VILLAGE
ANNUAL STEAM ENGINE

The word below the second line had been hastily erased, presumably with the side of someone's hand. Solly tried to remember what the missing word was, or the missing words. FESTIVAL? EXHIBITION? DEMONSTRATION? Or maybe something clever, like BLOWOUT. Didn't matter, though, because scrawled in white chalk beneath those two lines was:

SKUNK PROBLEM
AT THE
FOOD BOOTH

Solly licked his right index finger and reached toward the chalkboard. He carefully erased all the consonants from the third line in white chalk and stood back to read the whole sign again:

WELCOME TO PIONEER VILLAGE
ANNUAL STEAM ENGINE
SKUNK PROBLEM
AT THE
OO   OO

Maybe later he'd get rid of *all* the consonants. He was thinking that he probably had a lot of time to kill.

A shadow passed over Solly's eyes and he became aware of a faint flapping sound. Looking up, he saw a lone turkey vulture sailing across the cloudless sky. He watched it disappear into the distance like a single piece of punctuation in the corner of a sheet of blue paper.

His legs steady again, Solly started toward the parked cars. One licence plate, on a silver PT Cruiser, read: BEAN-IE 123. The grass, upon which he walked silently, looked perfectly groomed. The indentations the tires had made were invisible now. How many days does it take for that to happen? For the grass to regain its stature after it's crushed by a tire.

When he reached his car, Solly jammed a hand into his rear pocket. He pulled out the squished hamburger bun, transferred it to his other hand, and jammed the first hand back in. A tiny slip of paper. His raffle ticket for the quilt. He let it flutter to the ground. Now the pocket was empty. He felt the other pockets, patting against the black denim of his jeans, but they were empty, too. Solly found a large rock in the grass and began hammering at the driver's window of his car. This set off the car horn, and its bassoon-like honk blared across the field of cars at three-second intervals. When he'd finally smashed a hole in the window, Solly reached in and unlocked the door, swung it open, and slid behind the steering wheel.

The hamburger bun was dry and chewy. Somewhere in the car there was probably a little ketchup packet from a hamburger drive-through, but Solly couldn't be bothered to look. His life had changed.

Peering up through the windshield, he saw the turkey vulture winging back. It grew larger and larger. Did the turkey vulture know there'd been a whole thing with a skunk? Did it know what had become of Carla and Sim? And who would win the raffle?

There were plenty more buns on the shelves of the food booth. Eventually the car's battery would die and the horn would stop honking.

Solly would wait for his wife and son to show up, or for the results of the raffle to be announced. Whichever came first.

It was like living in another century.

His was the life of a pioneer.

HANOVER, 1959

The rain fell hard but only briefly; it had its usual effect. The streetcar rattled to its final halt. None were found within.

Questions for classroom or book-club discussion:

1. Did you feel you could relate to any of the characters in this novel? Who did you most closely identify with? Have you ever experienced anything similar in your lifetime?

2. Why did the author feel it was necessary to set the story in 1959?

3. Who built the streetcar? Are the Serbs to blame?

4. Does this remind you of any other novels you have read?

5. Who do you imagine playing the role of the rain if a film version were to be made of *Hanover, 1959*?

6. Do you feel trigger warnings should have been included at the front of this novel?

7. Virginia Woolf once wrote: "His wife was crying, and he felt nothing; only each time she sobbed in this profound, this silent, this hopeless way, he descended another step into the pit." Compare the use of the semicolon in this passage with the semicolon in the novel.

8. Why was the "halt" "final"?

9. Do you feel motivated to read more novels by this author?

10. Everyone has their own favourite passage from *Hanover, 1959*. What is yours?

EVIDENCE

A hammer lay on the floor. It didn't move. There was no wind, and had there been wind, it sure would have taken a lot of wind to move the hammer. But the hammer didn't budge. It was just the molecules that made up a hammer.

Three days went by. The hammer still hadn't moved. The fact of the passage of three days was proven only by the clock, because there was no change in the lighting. It wasn't like a sun went up and down. The clock sat on the floor, its back to the hammer. In a world where there were only clocks and hammers, one would measure distance like this: "The clock sat four hammers away from the hammer."

The clock had arms that moved. And stuff inside it that moved. Mechanisms. But nothing inside the hammer moved. It was just the molecules that made up a hammer. It did not know that three days had passed. That somewhere there was a sun, even though there was no evidence of a sun from where the hammer lay. It did not know it was confined. The clock, too—the clock did not know it was confined. It wasn't aware of the existence of the sun, of a thing called the sun.

Okay. A nose hurt. It was on a guy. That could be determined because when the guy stepped away from the wall, the nose went with him. Had the nose stayed on the wall, then it would be clear that walls had noses. The guy had arms that moved, and lower down he had legs, which also moved. Every part of the guy could move!

The guy stood nine hammers away from the hammer and five hammers away from the clock. The guy had an ambition in his head. The ambition was to be on the other side of the wall. But the hurting of his nose told him he could not simply walk through the wall. He couldn't walk through it now, just as he couldn't walk through it five minutes earlier. He was beginning to think that five minutes from now, when five minutes had passed, he would still be unable to walk through the wall.

The hammer had no ambition in its head. Therefore, it just lay there, just lay on the floor. The clock ticked, what with all its mechanisms. It became five minutes from now.

The guy reached into his pocket and withdrew a piece of yellow chalk. He drew a large X on the place on the wall that had hurt the nose on him. The X meant this was a place on the wall he could not walk through. The guy turned so his back was to the wall and his front was to the clock. The wall was zero hammers away from the guy, and the clock was still five hammers away.

The guy looked straight ahead. Beyond the hammer there was another wall, a wall covered in yellow X's. Because the guy's head could move, he looked to his left and to his right: more walls, more X's. Beyond these walls was a sun, the guy was almost certain of it. The sun was yellow, like the piece of chalk he held in his hand. The piece of chalk was very small. He remembered that once it had been much bigger.

The hammer remembered nothing. It just lay on the floor. The clock, too, remembered nothing. It could provide evidence that days had passed, but it remembered nothing. This meant, the guy reasoned, that there was no relation between time and memory.

The guy turned to his right and began to walk slowly. That new thought had energized him. The thing about time and memory. When the guy learned something new, it changed him. He was a changed man. Soon the guy's nose hurt again. He drew a yellow X, turned slightly to his left, and walked again. Each time his nose hurt, he drew a yellow X, adjusted his direction, and began walking again. The nose went with him. That meant that walls didn't have noses.

The hammer lay on the floor. It hadn't moved. The motion of the guy did not affect the motionlessness of the hammer. It simply kept not moving. It was just the molecules that made up a hammer. It learned nothing. It didn't change. It was unaware that beyond the walls was a sun, a sun the colour of chalk.

The clock, which had moving arms, and stuff inside it that moved, was also unaware of the sun beyond the walls. The clock was just the molecules that made up a clock.

The walls were another thing, a whole other story, even though they were just the molecules that made up a wall. On one side of a wall were yellow X's drawn in chalk. The abrasion of a guy's shoulder as he walked along the wall. The absence of time and memory. The absence of noses.

But on the other side of a wall was the heat of the sun, and the light that the sun threw upon the wall. Then time passed. Then the wall was dark and cool. Again, the passage of time. Soon the wall was warm and bright. Eventually: dark and cool.

Okay. And wind. On the side of the wall upon which the sun threw light, there was wind. It sure would take a lot of wind to move the wall. But the wall didn't budge. The wall changed continually, but it did not move and it remembered nothing. This meant there was no relation between motion and memory.

A wall is just the molecules that make up a wall.

THE UNITED STATES HAS GONE CRAZY

Behold. Here is a blender. Look at all the buttons and dials on it. Put stuff in it and turn it on. This is what the blender does: it takes solids and reduces them to something more manageable, encourages them to mingle. Carrots and potatoes. Ice cream and shards of chocolate. It takes two entirely different liquids and turns them into one all-new liquid. Coca-Cola and milk, for example. Beet juice and coconut rum.

Outside the window, a horse tugs a wagon down the street. The pale man on the wagon wears a tall black hat. He speaks to the horse almost without breathing, like he's ordering a coffee and toast after a sleepless night. I've never seen him before. He will come to be known as The Stranger. Especially when he rides into a new town, silent but for the clomping of horse hooves. The women of the town will peek at him through parted curtains. When he looks, his head barely turning, he'll see only the curtains swaying ever so slightly, as if stirred by a breeze.

Meanwhile, everyone's family is torn asunder. The brothers bicker over whether their cousin's child is a cousin once removed or a second cousin. Husbands and wives can't believe they've put up with each other for so long. They roll their eyes and grind their teeth. They clench their arthritic fists. The children refuse to pick the lice out of each other's hair. Grandfather hurls his false teeth into the fetid creek behind the cottage.

Then this: a whistling emanates from the sky. The United States has gone crazy and is bombing everyone again. All the other countries raise their gigantic metal domes, and it sounds like it's raining and you're sleeping in a room with a corrugated tin roof. You dream of broad-shouldered men who need to shave and whose sweat has soaked through their shirts. They lob explosives at each other, then tuck their heads beneath their arms. A parking lot has only one car in it, and the car is upside down. This is terror. This is what terror is.

The family boards a plane to fly across the ocean, to visit where Grandfather was born. Grandfather has trouble breathing and is attached to a machine, he has smoked too much, so he cannot go. An announcement is announced. There is a rat on the plane. A lady saw a rat in the aisle. The passengers are asked to look under their seats, but no one sees the rat. The passengers are asked to stomp their feet, so the noise and vibrations will drive the rat from its hiding place. The pilot fears that the rat has made its way into the plane's mechanism. The passengers are asked to leave the plane and to take all their personal belongings. The family goes home, and Grandfather won't let them in.

The Stranger ties his horse to a post and walks into an eatery. He sits on a stool at a wooden counter and asks for a coffee and six slices of toast, no butter. While he's waiting, he digs into his pocket, finds a scrap of paper, makes some notes on it. There is an enormous explosion outside, and the floor of the eatery trembles. The Stranger's writing hand veers off the scrap of paper, his pen gouging a trail through the wooden counter. He imagines what might happen if his hand just kept skidding away from him, off the counter, onto the floor, out the back door, and on toward whatever lies beyond, whatever lies beyond.

The retractable metal domes that cover the countries outside the American borders, both on the same continent and those more distant, were manufactured in the late 1990s by a company called NationHood Innovations. That's when they were manufactured, but they weren't installed until sometime later. It was tricky putting them up, but the engineers of the various countries showed rare cooperation and eventually succeeded. One columnist for the *Guardian* suggested, tongue-in-cheek, that each dome should have a trampoline mounted above it, so that the bombs would bounce right back toward the U.S., but this was considered in bad taste and he was fired the next day.

Grandfather can no longer eat solid foods, so his dinners are put in a blender before they are served. The children enjoy watching the meat loaf and celery turn to sludge. They want to put their own dinners in the blender. At lunchtime, they want to put their peanut-butter sandwiches in the blender. Grandfather's inability to eat solid foods has brought the family together in a meaningful way.

It is night, finally. The Stranger sits on a curb on a residential road, under the pale yellow glow of a street lamp. He is ruminating on the book he is writing. A huge rat tugs at one of his shoelaces, and The Stranger reaches out a bony finger and scratches the rodent's head. Every time a metallic thud sounds from above, man and rat flinch, they both flinch. The United States has done a lot of good things, particularly in the areas of literature and Cajun cuisine, but now it's gone crazy.

THE MAN WHO MISTOOK CLAUDE FRANÇOIS FOR BREATHING

for Stephen Ticktin

The patient entered my office looking very agitated. A Caucasian man in his mid-forties, about five-foot-nine, thin, prematurely grey hair, bags under his eyes, compromised posture. He wore a pair of slightly baggy blue jeans and a black shirt, the sleeves rolled up to midway between wrist and elbow. He repeatedly patted his shirt and pants pockets, even before sitting down in the chair I indicated. Was he a

chain smoker? I would eventually learn that he was searching for his phone, even though he had lost it several days
earlier, likely leaving it in a cab on his way to his mother's
funeral.

In quiet, staccato speech, he explained that he was having
trouble breathing, that he needed to gasp for air, and that
less and less of it was getting down into his lungs. He feared
he was dying and he would never see "the clip" again. It was
this clip that allowed him to breathe. I had received his case
folder from the hospital that morning, and so I knew that
this desperation about his breathing was strictly psychoso-
matic. In truth, he was breathing deeply, if a bit erratically.

I withdrew a small mirror from my desk and held it in front
of his mouth, so that he could see it fog up. "That is your
breath," I told him. He stared at it silently. And then I asked
him about this "clip"—was it a tie clip? The speed at which a
horse ran? A haircut?

The heaving of his chest slowed somewhat and the man gathered himself. He told me he would start from the beginning.
I raised my pen to my writing pad and told him to take his
time. I wanted to hear every detail.

It was nearly a decade ago that he first saw the clip. His girlfriend had unexpectedly broken up with him, and he was
devastated. A few months had passed, but it didn't seem to be
getting any easier. The loneliness he felt was profound. He

had always been shy around women, and he knew it might be a long time before he rallied the courage to date again. He was tidying up his house, which he said contained a few dozen metre-high stacks of newspapers he hadn't yet gotten around to reading, and he found himself humming a tune he recognized from his childhood. His enthusiasm began to rise as he told me the pattern of the song: *da, da, da, da-da, da-da*. He found himself humming the tune repeatedly for the next few days, and he made great headway with the newspapers, shaving a few centimetres off each pile and stuffing the rejects into his fireplace. His father had told him that newspapers were excellent for starting fires, but that he should never burn books, because that's what the Nazis did.

And then it struck him: *My father said to me one day...* That was the song! *...that girls, girls, girls are made to love.* Each day a few more of the lyrics came to him, and soon he was singing the song in its entirety. He had first heard it, he explained, when his older brother owned the 45 rpm single and occasionally played it on the turntable. He loved the song so much, he used to grab whatever cylindrical thing was at hand—a magic marker, one of his mother's curlers, a cucumber—and pretended it was a microphone and that he was the singer, and as the record spun, he mouthed the words and danced around the house.

Determined to hear the recording again, after so many years, he went to the public library, where he was told they had computers for patrons' use, and he typed in *girls girls girls* to see if he could find the song and who had sung it. But what came up in the search results was a link to a video called "Belles, Belles, Belles." He put on the pair of headphones provided with each computer in the library, and he played the video. A handsome blond man in a red sweater and black pants danced through the snow, accompanied by various attractive women who were also dancing. And the man in the red sweater was indeed singing the song this patient remembered from childhood, but the words he sang were French. The song lasted slightly more than two minutes, and he played it again and again, until his half-hour at the computer had run its course.

For the first time, he explained to me, he felt he could breathe again, the depression had lifted, he felt light and hopeful. Each day he came back to the library and played the video over and over. Sometimes he visited the library for half an hour in the morning and half an hour in the afternoon. The librarian, he said, seemed only slightly annoyed.

But the video demanded repeated viewings. Every time he watched it, he saw something he hadn't noticed before. It might have been the particular shade of mascara one of the women wore, or the detail of a dance move the singer performed that he hadn't seen earlier. It was only after weeks of watching this video that he allowed his eyes to drift down from the image and he saw the name of the singer below the frame. The singer's name was Claude François. The song was called "Belles, Belles, Belles." He translated that for me as "Beautifuls, Beautifuls, Beautifuls."

I asked the patient if he found the singer attractive, and, patting at his shirt and pants pockets, he confirmed that he found both the singer and the various women in the video attractive. He couldn't get enough of them, he explained. Soon he needed more than those half-hour blocks at the library.

He couldn't afford to buy his own computer, he had never owned one, but one of the librarians told him that he could buy a small phone and watch the clip of "Belles, Belles, Belles" on that device. He could watch it all day and all night. He didn't know if the librarian was trying to help him or to free up the public computer. But it didn't matter. Within a few weeks he had put together the sum of money necessary to buy the small phone.

The patient looked ecstatic as he related this to me. His breathing had calmed and his eyes seemed to shine. He said that now he could watch the clip whenever he wanted, at any time of day or night, just as the librarian had promised.

He soon left his job as night janitor at the local elementary school, because it interfered with his viewing of the clip. His elderly father began paying his rent, but the man would have to move into a smaller apartment, a more affordable one. He burned all his newspapers and gave away most of his belongings so that he could fit in the single room with a shared bathroom down the hall. What he lost in floor space, he explained, he gained in contentedness.

He no longer felt lonely. This, he said, was the golden age of his life. There was so much to absorb in that two-minute clip, he said, it could be a person's life work. He no longer even remembered the name of the young woman who'd broken his heart. For almost a decade, he clutched his small phone and played the clip over and over, stopping only to eat or nap. His mother, who by now was a widow, became distraught and her health began to decline. He told me this matter-of-factly, without emotion. And then he became exhilarated again as he told me about the last ten seconds of the clip, when Claude François and the women began throwing snowballs at each other. "While still dancing!" he nearly shouted.

And then it was as if he froze. His face sagged, and then his shoulders, and then his back and his limbs. He sank into the chair in my office as if he were a large stone thrown into a pond. Not because his mother was dead, but because, on the way to her funeral, he had lost his phone and could no longer watch the Claude François clip that had taught him to enjoy life again, to breathe.

I was about to ask why he hadn't simply purchased another phone, a strategy that seemed not to have occurred to him, but then I thought better of it. The last thing I should do was encourage his obsessive-compulsive behaviour. He was gasping now, flailing for air, patting again at his shirt and pants pockets. I asked him if he thought his phone might simply reappear in one of his pockets. He sobbed and continued searching for his lost phone. I explained to him that he didn't need the clip to breathe. But he only patted more frantically at his pockets, his eyes wide.

In his twenties, the patient had begun to obsessively save newspapers he didn't have time to read. These piles of newspapers took up much of the floor space in his apartment. It is unclear whether he ever caught up on a single edition. This may have led to the devastating breakup of his relationship with the unnamed woman. The newspaper-hoarding disorder was replaced, after two decades, by his compulsive viewing of the Claude François video of the 1960s French pop song "Belles, Belles, Belles." The patient left his job, and was supported then only by his parents and a small monthly stipend from the government, awarded when a previous psychiatrist determined he was unable to work.

When he lost his phone, he began compulsively patting the pockets of his various items of clothing, in hopes of finding it again, though he knew, consciously, that he had almost certainly left the phone in the taxi he took to his mother's funeral. Traumatic orphan-pocket disorder is not uncommon. The patient has suffered two enormous losses—the father and the mother—and he repeatedly pats his pockets, as if he has left something behind. What makes this case unique is that the deaths of his parents have been displaced by the loss of his phone, and thus the loss of the Claude François video.

The patient believed he was in my office not because he had once accumulated fifty metres of stacked newspapers in his home, nor because he had watched a French pop video tens of thousands of times, nor because he couldn't stop patting his pockets in search of his lost phone—he was here because he believed he couldn't breathe.

I needed at first to put his body at rest. I pointed out to him that he had only so many pockets and each pocket had only a finite amount of space, and that he had already confirmed the absence of the phone after many dozens of inspections. Was he able to gently put his hands on his lap and keep them there, for even ten minutes? He stilled for a moment, looked at me, and said, "But CloClo…" And then his hands again resumed their thorough investigations.

(Later research determined that "CloClo" was a name often used by fans of the singer Claude François to refer to their idol. During the 1960s, Mr. François rivalled the Beatles for popularity in France. He survived an attempt on his life and other near-death experiences. He died in a bathtub accident, just short of age forty. Mr. François was best known for co-writing the French ballad that would become "My Way" in English. He had a beautifully cleft chin.)

"Mr. R—," I said to the patient. "I ask you to lie on the floor on your back." He glanced at me, puzzled. I indicated the space on the floor between the chair in which he was seated and my own desk. The patient stood, patted his pockets one more time, and then lay down as I had asked. I asked him then to lay his arms at his sides and place his palms beneath his body, cupping the backs of his upper thighs. He did so.

I sat silently and observed him for ten minutes. His chest began to rise and fall more evenly. The sound of an industrious woodpecker filtered in through the window of my office. *Bang bang bang. Belles belles belles. Bang bang bang. Belles belles belles.* I glanced at my wristwatch. "Ten minutes have passed, Mr. R—, and you have not patted your pockets a single time. Claude François is still dead. The clip of him singing his song still exists. Your phone remains on the floor in the back of a cab. Your parents are dead. You are breathing."

At my home that evening, I re-enacted the patient's search on the internet. I typed *girls girls girls* into the search bar on my computer. My fingertip rested lightly on the Enter key. From outside, in my backyard, I heard *Bang bang bang. Belles belles belles. Bang bang bang. Belles belles belles.* That fucking woodpecker had followed me home.

I AM THE NEXT MICKEY FISCHBAUM

Your honour, I am not just the person standing before you. See the person standing before you? The two legs? The arms? A pair of eyebrows and a mouth? It is not just me. I am additional, supplementary. I am the next Mickey Fischbaum. The next Mickey Fischbaum. I am the next Mickey Fischbaum. The subsequent. I am mysterious and I am marvellous. I am the man. Where did I come from? I know not. I just appeared, mid-stride, walking down the street, past a hat shop and a broken fire hydrant. A gentleman walking in the opposite direction brushed against my elbow and muttered an apology. These were all new to me: strides, hats, hydrants, gentlemen, elbows, apologies. It was like someone across the road was pointing and said, "Let's invent a new person walking along—right *there*!" And I came into being. I materialized. I was suddenly manifested on the sidewalk. No history. No memory. But I was going somewhere. This is the thing: I have always felt propelled toward my destiny. I literally came into being as a man of action. A man. The next Mickey Fischbaum, your honour. Standing here before you.

And I'd like the jury to cast their eyes—all twenty-four, because I've inventoried the number of your eyes, self-taught in math—upon the me that is before you, and see, twenty-four times over, there is an additional me. A subsequent me. And Mickey Fischbaum, of whom I am the next, would say, "self-taught in math" is a dangling participle—it doesn't refer to your eyes, but to me. I would never have known that. I came into being mid-stride, without ever taking a lesson in math. Mickey Fischbaum would know that, but not me. I am merely an autodidact, so I know nothing except cars. And everything I know about cars, I taught myself, ladies and gentlemen of the jury. I am the man. I am the most sensational man. I am remarkable. I am the man. The next Mickey Fischbaum.

I will not deny that I am disappointed I did not win the Pulitzer Prize. Not for me, but for Burma, for the people of

East Timor, for those living in the slums of Burundi without a kopeck to their name. The gesture would have been so appropriate. Aren't we supposed to win prizes sometimes for the people we sometimes spend some time thinking about, those less fortunate than we are? Or for the even more generous thoughts we had, during prize season, several years earlier, when overlooked by our colleagues? The colleagues on the Pulitzer Prize jury. I say this not for myself, but for those who are not the next Mickey Fischbaum, who live with a burden that I myself do not have to bear.

It is not me in this courtroom, your honour, it is the next Mickey Fischbaum, and so the charges against me are the burden of the man who did the things that the person who is not the next Mickey Fischbaum did. Did I expose myself in the public washroom of the Newark Bus Terminal to an undercover police officer on New Year's Eve 1992? Did I pull the emergency stop cord of the F train at rush hour, sending an eighty-two-year-old man into fatal cardiac arrest? Did I urinate in the public fountain bearing the statue of Norman St. Vincent Edna Millay Peale as children threw nickels therein and made wishes? Perhaps the man you seek to try is not the next Mickey Fischbaum but a man who is the person who is not the next Mickey Fischbaum. Although robbed of the Pulitzer Prize, year after year, I am sensational. On a crowded sidewalk, one may ask, "Who is the man?" and it is I who steps forward, unjustly Pulitzer Prizeless, decade after decade, a slap in the face though that may be to the people of war-torn Honduras and countless other African nations crushed by their debt to the dictatorial trinity of Curly, Larry and Moammar Khaddafy.

Although I wear the bracelets of oppression around my slender ankles, I will turn one hundred and eighty degrees and walk out the door of this courtroom. I am the man. I am the man. I am the man. I am the height that I am, and the weight, and thus am the next Mickey Fischbaum. I have put the word *success* in the word *successor*, and see how my body pivots in place until I face the door, my back to you, your honour, and I shuffle slowly, see me shuffle, shuffle despite my shackles, slowly, toward the door that leads to my future. The jury will disregard the previous deliberations and decisions of the Pulitzer Prize jury, as well as your instructions and their own nightmares and all that they have learned. And you, your honour, you are left to find the man who urinated into the fountain and displayed his genitals to an undercover officer, as I bow my head and drive my entire fantastic self into the future, a future in which each breathing man, woman, and child on this earth welcomes me as the next Mickey Fischbaum.

LA PAPA

They're all over the sidewalks, and they've got their kids, and their old people, and guys with white canes, and children with crutches, they're spilling out over the curbs, right into the streets. It's like the street is a continuation of the sidewalk, or else everything is just a big field of grass, but really it's cement. They're orderly, patient, no jostling, moving like a gigantic flowing amoeba, and I'm caught up in the wave.

A buggy is coming down the road, I can just make out the driver in the distance, and the top of the horse's head, and the people are parting for it, but reaching for it, too. As it gets closer, I see that the buggy is drawing a wagon, and around the wagon, sitting on the edges, their legs hanging over like stalks of wilted celery, are men with rifles. They've got rifles resting across their laps, but they look really friendly.

Men and women are reaching out toward the wagon, and kids on the shoulders of the men and women, they're reaching out, too. Their arms are outstretched, and their fingers are trying to telescope further, but they don't have telescopic fingers, not in this town. It was the first thing I noticed. Some of their hands are reaching past the heads of the men with rifles. But the men with rifles just tilt their heads out of the way, they're okay with it, they see no threat.

From the distance, maybe a couple streets over, comes music, or perhaps it's music fading away, disappearing further, toward the lake. What we're hearing is the residual sounds of marching songs, delicate residual melodies, individual notes, wafting in the air like autumn leaves that have—that have fallen off a tree, right? So there's this sense of dissipating celebration. But the people are focused on the wagon, not on the distant, fading music. And as the wagon is nearly in front of me, I see that it holds an enormous replica of a microwave oven. It's a terrible replica, like something an untalented child might have made for a school project: the oven itself is made of corrugated cardboard, and the dials and buttons and door and stuff are all painted on in wobbling poster paint.

A man who has climbed a lamp post and is thus perched at a level higher than the cardboard microwave, points and shouts, "The Potato!" There is a wave of excitement in the crowd and then everyone falls silent. It is as if those two words are a magic spell. On giant screens set up in the intersection, an image begins to manifest itself. At first it is blurry, and then we can make out a shrivelled oblong blob of orangey brown. If it is a potato, it is very, very old. I can almost smell the mould growing on it. The woman beside me says to the woman beside her, "It is noticeably older this year than it was last year." And thus I learned that for those who saw the potato last year, before I'd arrived in this town, they could recognize that the potato had aged. It was more withered than it had been last year. It smelled worse. Those stringy white growths that used to scare me when I was a kid and I stumbled on a sweet potato mouldering in the dank cupboard under the kitchen sink, they were longer than they were twelve months ago, like the wild beard of a prophet.

"How long," I asked the woman, "has the potato been—umm—"

"In charge?" she finished for me.

"Yes, how long has the potato been in charge?" I gazed back at the big screen and the blob projected thereon.

She looked at me with curiosity, or perhaps it was sympathy. It was clear I was from away. "It was rescued from the microwave oven in the basement of the Bank of the Horrible Currency three days after the quake. The microwave was still on, its interior glowing, even though there was no power in the town. The door was jammed and firemen had to rescue the Potato with an axe."

The wagon had come to a complete stop now. The horses snorted and whinnied, frightened by the serene accumulation of arm-stretchers. A small biplane flew overhead, a white banner with black lettering flapping in its wake: "It's The Potato." The mob paused momentarily, looking up, cupping their hands at their brows, waving at the pilot or the banner or the propeller. One couldn't be certain exactly what they were waving at.

"The Potato had been in the microwave," continued the woman, "for three days, cooking. And yet it was still plump and fibrous and moist and orange. It was the very vitality of the Potato itself that must have kept the microwave oven operating even in the absence of electricity."

"The quake?" I asked. "When was it? If you don't mind my saying, the potato looks a bit older now. Less plump, you know?"

The woman smiled gently. "You're not from here, I thought so. The quake devastated our town eleven years ago. Everything had to be totally rebuilt: the houses, the town hall, the water filtration plant, the bowling alley, the police station—everything. And the Potato personally directed all the construction. The responsibility has taken a toll on it."

I nodded my thanks and extricated myself from the crowd. Soon the potato would be little more than a hard pebble, or the desiccated corpse of a baby mouse. Like when you find one covered in a tight cloud of dust in the corner of the kitchen, a child poking at it with a stick and whimpering.

Back at my apartment, blocks from the main street, I sat at my window, my forehead pressed against the pane. Had the potato chosen a successor yet? What would happen when the potato was spent? Who would maintain order? Would this soon be once again a ghost town?

On the street below, a dog came trotting into view. It pushed its snout at a sewer grate, snapped at a low-swooping bird, started chasing its tail. There was no way I could see this dog as the potato's successor. Nor the plastic bag sailing by on a breeze. Nor my left shoe or my toothbrush or the smoke trickling skyward from the crumbling chimney across the road.

It was almost as if I'd just arrived, and already I was packing again. I stuffed a suitcase full of my clothes and my papers and my photographs, photographs of family members whose names I no longer remembered. I had only a few books, mostly tattered novels in Portuguese, a language I could barely read, or maybe it was Serbo-Croatian, I'm not sure, and these I crammed into my knapsack.

It was the days before the invention of everything, a very long time ago. The winds were warm and they called your name. The roads were thick with crickets that crunched beneath your feet. Deer watched you from the thickets, their glistening noses twitching. Now I lie in front of my father's weathered headstone and I read. Each page I finish, I know I will never read again. At night, a woman comes to tuck me in, the number of blankets varying with the season. In the morning, a man brings me a tin bowl filled with stew. Although it is barely enough to see me through the day, I share it with the guy in front of the next headstone, who is not so lucky.

HOUSING

for Ashley Barker

I'll eat your house. I'll eat your house, and then you'll have nowhere to live. Where will you put your books and your bicycle? Where will you put your winter coat? Your jar of dried lentils? The framed photograph of your mother standing beside Carol Channing at the opening of *Gentlemen Prefer Blondes*? I will not eat your house because I am hungry, nor out of any ill will I harbour toward you. I will not eat your house because it was poorly constructed, nor because it is in violation of any by-laws, nor because it stands in the path of a highway I'd like to build.

I do not know the number on your front door nor the street on which your house stands. You have never invited me to your house.

I will don my bib and wander the streets. My bib bears a picture of a lobster wearing a bib bearing a picture of a lobster. It will protect me from getting any bits of house on the front of my shirt. If I ate your house, then went into work with bits of house on the front of my shirt, my boss would not be pleased. It would be inappropriate for me to enter my workplace wearing my lobster bib with a lobster bib.

To enter the building where I work, I am equipped with a card with a magnetic stripe. I have put a Post-it note on the card, and the Post-it note says: REMOVE BIB.

But I have a fear. I fear that as I approach my workplace, one of my workmates will at the same moment be leaving, and she will hold the door open for me, and so I won't need my card with the magnetic stripe to get in and will therefore not see the Post-it note I wrote for myself. She would only open the door for someone she knew, so I must ensure that she doesn't recognize me. I will buy a rubber face mask that has been designed to look like the face of an unpopular politician or a television celebrity. The woman will therefore not recognize me, and so she will close the door behind her, and

I will need my striped card to enter and will see the Post-it note, and if I am wearing my bib I will remove it.

Although I have told no one about my plans to eat your house, many people have approached me to ask me how I am going to eat your house. It's possible that you told them, but I don't know how you knew, because I only just told you sixty seconds ago.

This is how I had planned to eat your house. Originally, I had planned to eat your house from the foundation up. But then, I realized, the house would collapse on me. I didn't need to be an engineer to figure that out. And I am not an engineer. You do not want your house to collapse on me and I do not want your house to collapse on me. If it was a cartoon house, it is possible that I could begin eating it from its foundation up, and if I ate fast enough, it would hover in the air until I finished eating, and then there would be a little puff of smoke drifting into the sky. Because your house is not a cartoon house, I cannot begin with the foundation.

A house has a top so that rain cannot get in. I could eat your house by starting at the top. For this, I would need to bring a ladder or else find a ladder in your garage, if your house has a garage. One of the notable things about tops of things is that they are high. I, as a person, am very frightened when it comes to heights. I will not be eating your house starting from the top.

You heard me right. I will not eat your house starting from the top, because the top is high, nor will I eat your house starting from the bottom, because of the collapsing issue due to your house not being a cartoon house.

Phone calls, telegrams, and letters to the editor of some of the most prominent journals are all asking the same thing: what will be my strategy for eating your house?

And I say, why don't they ask instead where you will live once I have eaten your house? Will you remain in the city or will you move elsewhere? Will you take your few belongings and board a bus? Will you find a remote patch of beach and settle in to start a new civilization there? A civilization marked by empathy and compassion, one where people don't step on the heads of others so that they may benefit at the expense of their fellow citizens. A civilization where each person is guaranteed a basic living stipend and where labourers and artists can walk side by side in dignity, and not have to forage for potato peelings that have not yet gone mouldy. Where free health care and free education are guaranteed for all. *Lost in Space* plays on every television, followed by *My Mother the Car* and *Mr. Terrific*. This is the sort of civilization you could nurture, if only you would take responsibility for your own decisions and for the eating of your house.

When I eat your house, I will eat it respectfully and thought-fully. Don't concern yourself with whether I start from the bottom or from the top. You've got enough on your plate.

SQUEAK SQUEAK

I am sitting on a red balloon the size of a beanbag chair. The man with the camera stands perfectly still in front of me. He is wearing a T-shirt with a faded picture of Jim Morrison on it, and a pair of torn blue denim pants. I am wearing cut-off jeans myself, and my thighs are squeaking against the red balloon's taut surface. My hands rest on the balloon, palms down. When he asks, or gestures, I raise a hand and massage my breasts through the black bra I'm wearing. He has told me to keep rocking, gently, on the balloon. That's the key, apparently. The very gentle thrust of my pelvis as I rock on the balloon. It's a bit like being on a hobby horse.

An hour ago I came in through the revolving door of this building, six floors down, carrying a cup of tepid coffee in one hand, and a gym bag over my shoulder. I'd stuffed the ad in the back pocket of the black slacks I had on. The ad, which I'd clipped from the classifieds of the local entertainment weekly, said, "Young model wanted for short films: balloons, heels, etc."

When I was a child, I used to rub balloons against my hair and stick them on the wall of the rec room in our basement. This was all about static electricity. The same thing that sent a jolt through my finger if I touched the TV after walking across the carpet in my running shoes. The balloons would cling to the wall, and each day they'd become smaller, until they were just little runt balloons, and then they dropped to the floor like birds that had smacked into an office tower.

The balloons I stuck to the wall were invariably left over from a birthday party. Sometimes they had graphics on them: noisemakers, stars, streamers, candles. When I think of balloons, I think of pink and blue icing, and little flower blossoms made of sugar that crunch when you bite into them. I think of photographs of kids gathered around a table in the rec room, and maybe one kid blowing out the candles on a cake.

After I've rocked on the big red balloon for half an hour, the man with the camera hands me a pair of shiny pantyhose and a pair of spike-heel shoes and asks me to put them on. I'm surprised when he doesn't watch me change. He turns around and makes notes on a pad of lined paper, then plays with the settings on his camera. When I've slipped into the new clothes, I clear my throat and he turns around.

I'm wearing my black bra, the shiny pantyhose, and the black heels. He quickly looks me up and down and hands me a small heap of colourful uninflated balloons, then directs me to the bed in the corner of the room. *I want you to sit on the edge of the bed and slowly blow those balloons up*, he says. *The more you can make them make squeaking noises, the better. Also, blow them up so that they are so big they are just about to pop—but don't pop them. Not yet.* He is breathing heavily, like some obscene phone caller. He keeps patting the chest pocket on his shirt, as if he's looking for a pack of cigarettes.

Sitting on the edge of the bed, I pace myself, because it takes a lot of energy to blow up a balloon, and I don't want to get dizzy. The man is moving slowly around the bed, document-ing my every puff. Soon he is kneeling in front of me, shoot-ing me from below. The balloon must be obscuring my face entirely. The man seems almost agitated, but somehow he is, at the same time, steady with the camera and very professional.

After I inflate each balloon, I rub it in my hands, make it squeak, press my face against it, and sometimes even lick it. This is my own improvisation. The balloons glisten where I have licked them. The taste of the balloon against my tongue gives rise to another burst of nostalgia. I used to do this—I used to lick balloons—back when I was a child. My spit would get on them.

When all the balloons are inflated, the man instructs me to recline against the big pillows on the bed and lift the balloons one at a time, pressing them between my thighs, my knees, my calves, then pressing the heels of the shoes I'm wearing against the balloons. The balloons squeak like enthusiastic mice, and then they pop. The man lets out a small groan each time a balloon vanishes into mid-air. *This is really good,* he says. *They'll be cumming all over the walls when they see this.*

Sometimes when the balloons pop, they just collapse on the bed between my legs. Sometimes they hiss off to one side or another. They make that fleeting *whoosh* sound I remember, again, from childhood. All my thoughts of balloons are connected to my childhood. So it's difficult for me to imagine that men are going to watch these movies and they are going to masturbate, their faces turning red, sweat prickling on their brows and on their necks and on their palms.

I wonder whether they would blow their loads if it was just me, lying here on the bed, in my bra and pantyhose and heels. Or do they need the balloon? Am I just an accessory to the balloon? I remember when I was a teenager and I was walking in Parkdale with some girlfriends and our boyfriends. There were a few women on the street, trying to catch the attention of drivers. They wore thigh-high leather boots, some of them, and miniskirts, or spandex leggings, and small jackets over tight T-shirts or tank tops. One of them cradled a teddy bear in her arms. A guy I was with sauntered up to her and asked, *How much?* He paused. *I mean, just for the bear.* I felt sorry for the woman. Life was probably hard enough without some college kid making a stupid joke. She told him to fuck off. She wasn't going to pimp her teddy bear.

When all the balloons are popped, the man with the camera asks how I'm doing, and if I'm game for more. I tell him that if he is going to keep paying me, then I'm willing to continue. He gets up and reaches into a half-size fridge, gets out a couple of saran-wrapped sandwiches, and hands one to me. *Need your strength for this!* he says. The sandwich is egg salad on whole wheat bread. He has the same thing. We sit in silence, unwrap our sandwiches, and take long, slow chews. He hands me a can of ginger ale to help wash down the pasty filling.

When I come back from using the washroom, where I had to peel the shiny pantyhose down onto my thighs to get anything accomplished, he hands me a new outfit, a white turtleneck, black panties and black stockings. He asks me to take off my bra before I pull the turtleneck on. Then he turns around and writes again on his lined-paper pad, fiddles a little with his camera.

This time he wants me to talk. I ask if he has a script. He says, *Just say things like, "You like this balloon, don't you? Do you want me to pop this balloon? Do you want me to rub it on my tits? Do you want to press your cock against this balloon?" Stuff like that.* I thought I was only going to have to pose and I didn't expect to have to talk. But I'm willing to give it a try. I like the feel of the tight turtle-neck shirt, snug around my throat, across my breasts, and on my belly.

The man hands me a long hot-dog-shaped blue balloon and asks me to go out into the hallway so he can shoot me walking in through the door. When I get in I'm supposed to stop and stand there with my legs spread a bit and then start talking. Out in the hallway, a woman is trying to make a key fit into the lock a few doors down. She looks over at me and I smile, holding the balloon up in greeting. When the man calls from the other side of the door, I walk through, close the door behind me, and stand there with my legs a little beyond shoulder-width apart. He's holding the camera steady, and I hear the nearly imperceptible *whirr* as he shoots a close-up of my face. He nods, which means I should start talking.

For twenty minutes I talk to the men who will be watching this video. I make the balloon squeak, and I gently stroke it like it's a big blue penis. I ask the men if they like the balloon, if they want me to press it between my thighs, if they want to rub their cocks against it—*But be sure not to make it pop!*—and if they want me to lick the end of it, suck on the little twisted knot. I ask them if they are happy. If they like me for who I am as a human being. I ask them if they are content with the way things are in this country: with the distribution of wealth, the treatment of visible minorities, the government's response to global climate change. Do they think the lives of the poor on other continents are as valuable as our own lives here, where we have a hundred different soft drinks to choose from? Will they take a strong stand against factory farming. *I want you to cum*, I tell them. *Blast your hot, spewing cum all over the walls and the ceiling. It's the only way we're going to change society*, I explain. I turn around and bend over, feeling the panties ride into the crack of my ass, peering at my audience from between my legs, sawing the long blue balloon between my thighs. Upside down like that, I start to feel a little dizzy, the way I did when I was a child blowing up a balloon. At one birthday party, not mine but a friend's, a clown was there and he twisted the balloons into all sorts of animals: dogs, bunnies, giraffes, hippos. He gave each of the children an animal. I got the giraffe.

On the bus home, I have one hundred and twenty-five dollars in my pocket. I also have a few balloons in there. I look at the men sitting nearby, and the men standing, holding on to the straps above. Some of them glance at me, then glance away. Not one of them suspects that I have balloons in my pocket. But every one of them is thinking about balloons, I'm certain of it.

I look out the window. Everything passes by so quickly. A monkey is hawking pumpkins by the curb. A group of men in long scarlet robes are standing in front of the dry cleaners, their arms outstretched toward the clouds. On the steps of the police station, a woman stands on another woman's shoulders, reading a book and licking her fingertip each time she turns the page.

This is the way my life has changed: in the past, I used to eat egg-salad sandwiches with a glass of milk. Now, whenever I eat an egg-salad sandwich, I open a can of ginger ale. I hold it in my hand and it goes *squeak squeak*.

LEE MARVIN, AT YOUR SERVICE

There was a time, and it feels like yesterday, but really it was an era of Cold War paranoia and black dial phones and colour-TV-as-novelty, when it seemed like everywhere you went, every corner you turned, Lee Marvin was there, ready to give you a hand.

You would flood the engine of your car, and you'd sit there in your driveway, still pumping away at the pedal, and a song by Paul Revere and the Raiders would be squeaking out of your tinny radio speaker, and there'd be a knock at your window. You'd crank the window down, that's how you did it in those days, you'd crank your window down and peer up into the sunlight, and a tall figure would blot out the sun like there was some goddamn eclipse or something. And before you could say, "Are you Ray Walston from *My Favorite Martian*?" the giant silhouette with a brush cut would say, "Lee Marvin, at your service." And within minutes, seriously, you'd be picking up your date and you'd both go five-pin bowling.

Maybe your father would die, or no, your grandmother who lived in the family room and didn't know any English, spoke only Russian, but she made a great snack by frying up chicken fat and onions, and the whole family would sit in front of the Marvellous Invention of Colour TV and watch *Laugh-In* while dipping into the greasy bowl Grandma had prepared. And now she was gone, and you've all just come home from the funeral, and Solly says, "We'd better cover all the windows," and Sarah says, "No, we have to take the pillows off the bed and paint Jewish stars on all the mirrors," and Dad says, "Everyone take off your shoes and put on slippers or flip-flops." But really, no one had ever paid attention before to what you had to do when you were sitting shiva, because it had only ever been other people's shivas. And then there was a knock at the door, and when Mom answered, a tall blond man with muscular front teeth would poke his head inside and say, "Lee Marvin, at your service." And before you knew it, you'd have all the Jewish mourning customs down pat, and Lee would be leading the minyan in the Kaddish.

Same with if you were in a bank and lining up for the teller and you were confused by how to fill out the deposit slip, or if some skinny hood was robbing the bank, or if two kids in striped shirts were yelling at each other in the school-yard, or if you were short a few pennies when you were buying a pack of cigarettes or a bottle of cream soda, or if you had trouble making one of those cardboard pinhole viewers when there was a solar eclipse—next thing you knew, before you had even begun to panic: "Lee Marvin, at your service." That familiar square-jawed grin, the big hand reaching out to shake your own more mortal hand—"Lee Marvin, at your service"—and then he'd do his thing, it would take only a second, and everything would be better and you'd be on your way and the grilled-cheese sandwich wouldn't even have gotten cold yet, if there was a grilled-cheese sandwich involved in the situation.

But it's not like Lee Marvin didn't have his own problems. Lee Marvin had plenty. Just ask Jane Fonda, or Jean Seberg, or John Cassavetes. Or, if you don't like people whose names begin with the same letter as Jesus, ask Angie Dickinson. Anyway, this all happened so long ago, it's like it was another lifetime. I've put on weight, my hair is white now, and when I get my picture taken, it always looks like I'm lying in a coffin, like when Polly, our Latvian cleaning woman, showed us a photograph of her husband back in Latvia, and he really *was* lying in a coffin. We caught Polly stealing some of Mom's jewellery, and that was the end of Polly in our home. She wasn't very good anyway—sometimes we'd find cobwebs up near the ceiling after she left.

Our next cleaning woman was Clara, and Clara was from Argentina, and she never stole anything, not even if we deliberately left something out to test her. That's the difference between Latvians and Argentinians. Also, when Clara found my *Playboy* collection hidden under my bed, she didn't tell my parents. She just put the magazines in order by year and month and straightened out the stack. Bruce Jay Friedman, who is a very good writer—I've read four of his novels—used to write for *Playboy*. I always noticed what a Jewish name he had on top of his articles. I was surprised to see Jewish people writing in a magazine with nudie girls. My favourite Playmate was a lady from Hoboken, New Jersey. I think she's selling real estate now.

The thing about selling real estate is you have to really love what you're doing, because only genuine enthusiasm will compel someone to fork out the kind of money you need to fork out to own your own house. And you have to be able to look at the bright side of things—you have to always find the rainbow in the goddamn bug-infested swamp. If you lose your excitement about selling real estate—like, if you were really good but now there's no challenge left—it's time to do something else. People who don't think positively can't sell real estate. Sure, they might be able to sell a ramshackle bungalow here and there, but they could never be really successful. They should go into a business they can be more passionate about, like owning a hardware store or testing makeup products on animals.

The best Bruce Jay Friedman novel, according to me, is *Stern*. The former Playmate from Hoboken, New Jersey, is Janet Lupo.

May I suggest that you schedule an appointment with a career counsellor? These are people who come in all shapes and sizes, and they can make a genuine difference in your life. They may not be able to guarantee you a job, but they can help steer you toward the kind of professional pursuit that you are qualified for, and that you would find meaningful. Something you can really get behind.

Some think that a meaningful job is one that affects a lot of people, such as coming up with an important and complex theory like Einstein did, or being a prime minister, or becoming a police officer in a bad neighbourhood who really connects with the young people and encourages them to get meaningful jobs instead of being hoodlums and layabouts. A meaningful job might only be meaningful to the person who has the job, but that is enough. Meaningfulness is not measured by quantity. Being a meaningful job means being meaningful to the person who holds the job: it gives them self-respect and a purpose in life. It might just be playing a particular chord on a pipe organ at 2:00 p.m. once a year on the same date. It might be laying pipe for the delivery of oil. It might be sitting on a porch in a pioneer village smoking a corncob pipe like you were from the 1840s.

Early in 1840, the first issue of the American magazine *Electro-Magnet Intelligencer* was published. It appeared on January 18. On the same date, but in 1961, the lie detector was first employed in the Netherlands. That is incorrect. Another interesting fact about the Netherlands is that one in three Dutch people belong to a sports club, plus approximately three hundred castles in Holland are open to the public. These are "fun facts." You will find many more "fun facts" sprinkled throughout other stories that I have written.

FOOT WITHDRAWAL

after Benjamin Peret

The horizon, stretching from the glittering lake to the march of the splendid mountains in the distance, was lined with jars of pickled onions, their contents gently bobbing. Everyone who passed me on the street looked like a little red fish, a fish contented, smartly dressed in a diaphanous negligee of algae—straight out of a children's picture book. I ran my fingers through my spider-leg hair and checked for the fifteenth time that day to make sure my fly was zipped up. I tapped the slider with my fingertip and heard it buzz.

Inside the First Octagonal Bank of Our Lady of Perpetual Discrepancy, the teller—a handsome, dark-haired woman in her forties with gobs of mascara and a bob cut—looked at me with something hovering between suspicion and sympathy, and I looked at her with something I was certain was a profound love. I looked at her, but I kept my eyes averted, and so I had to look at her with my ear. I was relieved that I had trimmed my helix, tragus, and lobule that very morning. I looked at her with my ear.

"My foot?" I said.

The light in the great hall of the First Octagonal dimmed softly and a discordant orchestral swell arose behind her—was it César Franck?—as she sang her response in a voice I heard so often in my dreams. "Sorry?" Just that one word.

I cleared my barren throat. "I've come for my foot," I repeated. "What have you done with my foot?" I tried to summon the boldness to look up into her dark, oceanic eyes with my own, but my intention was struck by a riderless horse and wagon that veered sharply and sped off down a dank back alley, hooves clattering and wheels squawking.

"And you are," she sang, as hyacinths bloomed among the strands of her hair, "who you say you are?"

And that's when I felt the sharp munching sensation in the flesh of my scalp. Some large insect, I deduced, or some tiny animal. In any case, something with fine metallic teeth and a frenetic hunger for brain. I fought to resist flinching, lest I look like a lunatic before this Mysterious Goddess of Currency and Investments. And when I could no longer remain still beneath her piercing gaze, I worked my twitches into an anarchic cloud of avant-garde choreography that took me to every corner of the great bank floor. The other clients—both those hoarding millions and those seeking pennies—stepped to the peripheries and applauded, and several of them held up small devices with which, I was told later by a police officer, they recorded my every movement.

"I am Zalman," I told her, holding out my left hand. "Behold the telltale scar on the side of my thumb. It became part of me thirty years ago, when I acted all the roles in *A Doll's House* for my drama class at high school. Torvald strode from the room holding an enormous carrot on a platter and his thumb was ripped by a nail protruding from the door frame. Do you love the Scandinavians as much as I do?" I asked, placing the word love carefully in my sentence, to see, with my own ear, how she might react.

The teller, no doubt overcome with emotion, maintained her calm air and opened a small drawer to riffle through a file of well-thumbed index cards. "Thumb scar, thumb scar, thumb scar," she aria'd, "thumb scar, thumb scar— Ah, here we are: *Razovsky; thumb scar; Ibsen; door frame.*"

At last I looked up into her eyes, two undulating pools of seductive squid ink.

"Mr. Razovsky," she continued, adagio, "our records indicate that you yourself withdrew your foot in 1990. It is no longer in the bank's possession. We are footless. Your account is closed."

Tentacles of pain rippled through my back, then lunged up into my skull. The image I had conjured of this magnificent woman and me reclining by the Danube and reading to each other the whimsical sketches of Peter Altenberg vanished in a cartoon puff of smoke. "Why are you doing this to me?" I asked. "I'm only human."

"My great-grandfather, the late Percy Condor van Horowicz, founded this bank in 1861," the teller whispered in a Franckian anti-melody. "He had been saved by a benevolent octopus after a tragic shipwreck that wiped out his entire crew, and he swore that from then on, he would guard the people's money in a bank with as many walls as an octopus has arms to perform life-saving miracles. He wooed and then married Sophie-Marie Filament, a mid-level burlesque performer known for her extraordinary contortional talents, and together they fulfilled his dream. I, Sylvie-Marie, am named for her. We have the same eyes.

"Sophie-Marie's brothers-in-law, Mako and Sako, who performed as the Astounding Skullless Wonders in a travelling carnival and menagerie, had accumulated a great deal of money, and this they invested into what would become the First Octagonal Bank. Over the generations, they and their descendants protected the precious savings of many thousands of people. This grand edifice held pesos, dollars, francs, yen, quetzales, rubles, dinars, krones, takas, shekels, and more.

"Until 1989, that is, when you walked through these very doors and deposited your foot. This pedal extremity was kept under a physician's watch in a safety deposit box filled with formaldehyde and mint leaves, which were replenished weekly by local schoolchildren. The next year, without explanation, you returned to withdraw it and close your account."

The teller gazed at me dispassionately but not unkindly. I had stopped breathing.

"So, Mr. Razovsky, we no longer have your foot. I encourage you to peer down the length of your leg and discover it there."

I could barely catch my breath, let alone tilt my head down to peer toward the distant village of extremities. Was this woman, the great-granddaughter of the bank's founder, expressing for me her love, but doing so not in the typical, literal fashion?

My toes curled. Luckily, I had clipped their straining nails that very morning. I entered a state of mindfulness and counted. One toe curling, two toes curling... Yes, ten toes curled within my leather shoes, neither one more nor one less.

"My shoes," I said, "were handmade in Trieste by—"

We all threw ourselves to the floor as tiny explosions erupted in the bank's great hall, and the acrid-sweet scent of gunpowder filled the stale air. There were shouts, footfalls, the overturning of chairs. I sensed this was the end for me. I had never read an entire book by Dostoevsky. My little dog, Krapp, was waiting for me to return home and give him a treat. I had yet to watch "Desperate Minutes," the final episode of *My Mother the Car*, first aired on April 5, 1966.

The metallic teeth finally penetrated my skull and I could feel them pricking at my brain. I was lying on the floor, peering at the base of the bank counter, and on the other side of the counter lay Sylvie-Marie, the woman I loved. I adored her and I trusted her. I could feel her trying to communicate with me through the wooden base of the counter. I looked down toward my ankles and saw that, to each, a foot was indeed attached. Just as she had promised.

One of the robbers took centre stage on the bank's vast floor and began to declaim, and a sound like the repeated clicking of a trigger accompanied his speech. "Listen to me, and listen carefully. A caper may defined as a leap performed in a state of frolic. In this way, I caper about among your inert, prostrate bodies.

"A caper may be defined as an escapade that is ill-advised or perhaps even contrary to the law. In this way, each one of you is the victim of a caper.

"A caper may be defined as the bud of the shrub of the same name, but known to biologists as the *Capparis spinosa*."

I knew this was my moment. Whatever happened now would define me for the remainder of my life. I pulled myself to my feet, for both my feet were affixed to my ankles, just as I had been informed by the great-granddaughter of the sister-in-law of Mako and Sako, the men with no skulls, and someone once said that if you introduce a foot in act one it must be used in act three, and I pivoted toward the voice of the robber, preparing to kick him and thereby save the clients and staff of the First Octagonal.

But I saw only a jar of pickled onions. It stood among a row of identical jars, but it was clear which one had just spoken.

A bell chimed. A door squeaked open. Amid the echo of these two sounds, a voice bellowed, "Razovsky!"

It was my father-in-law, Ismail Horowicz. Sylvie-Marie stepped out of the back room at that moment, her arms filled with squirming jars of pickled asparagus.

"Issy!" I said. "You look fantastic! Convalescence has treated you well."

"This, my dear Zalman," he laughed, "is a very important day."

Sylvie-Marie and I looked at each other. Was this the first anniversary of the day we opened the doors of our modest shop, You Can Pickle Everything But A Screwdriver?

"This...is the first day of the rest of our lives."

First a chorus of gasps. Then a pandemic of applause rippled through the audience in the small theatre. Chairs scraped as the crowd rose to their feet as one. The small ensemble in the musicians' pit played a concluding flourish from Franck's *Le chasseur maudit* and, because this wouldn't be life if each thread was not resolved, I looked down at my foot and I mouthed a tiny thank-you.

THE "WIFE" OF CLAUDE FRANÇOIS

"Hello? Yes? Yes, this is Geneviève. What? What did you just say? You say that CloClo is dead? You say that he died in his hotel room? In the bathtub? It can't be! I just sent him a letter two days ago! I said that I love him and I love his music and I think that he's beautiful. I drew an ornamental border around the letter with gold and red pens, and blue pens and green pens.

"I just sent him the letter two days ago. What day is today—Wednesday? I sent it Monday. Do you think he received it? It took me weeks to write the letter. I wanted every word to be just perfect but also for my handwriting to be perfect and graceful. Because CloClo is perfect and graceful and he deserves nothing less!

"What is that, Simone? You say that thousands of people are pouring into the streets of Paris? Holding candles? Holding photographs of him? There must be some kind of mistake—I just sent my letter to him two days ago! On Monday! I told him that I have all his records, and that my older sister gave me his records from when she was a kid. I am a member of his fan club, and I'm the official secretary of his fan club for my village. If people want to join his fan club, they have to ask me. So far there is only me in my village. Do you know how lonely it has been being the only one who loves CloClo? It's not like Paris here. It's not like a big city. We don't have any arrondissements. We don't even have a record store! We share the cemetery with the next village over.

"Already the tears are streaming down my face. Can you hear them? I am pacing in circles around my room and I am looking at the walls and on all four walls I see CloClo's perfect face. I have posters of him on all my walls. His beautiful eyes. His lips that I kiss every day before I go to school. His bouquet of hair that I caress. What? You say Paris has come to a standstill? People are spilling from the shops, cafés, and offices? Girls are throwing themselves off buildings in grief?

"Sometimes I play that I am the wife of Claude François. We are very much in love. I make a beautiful home for us. It is a modest cottage but I make it look like the most majestic castle. And soon we will have children, did I tell you? A little blond boy and a little blond girl, they are so cute, as you can imagine. The girl is Alexandra and the boy is Alexandrie. The girl wears a shiny silver dress and the boy wears a shiny silver suit. Oh, they are adored by *everyone* at school!

"CloClo brings me gifts from each of the cities he visits when he is on tour. He brings me necklaces and handbags and exquisite dolls, you must see them sometime. I cook him dinner and he always compliments the dishes I prepare. His eyes sparkle as he cleans off his plate. You see, he must have good food to give him all the energy he needs so that he can dance with the Clodettes. I have about a million cookbooks in our gigantic, gleaming kitchen, but I never need to use them—I know exactly what dishes will make him happy, right out of my head.

"I feel like he will walk through the door any minute now! He will scoop up our darling children in one arm and embrace me with the other. I will feel his strong full lips against my forehead. I prepare a cocktail for him before dinner and we all go into the living room, where he settles himself into our enormous plush sofa. A child sits on each of his handsome knees. He has had such a hard day rehearsing that he just wishes to unwind. One of the Clodettes sprained her ankle, and it has been extra work to train her replacement.

"You say that police sirens are filling the streets of Paris? That a chorus of 'Comme d'habitude' is rising into the sky above the city? You say that you can barely catch your breath between sobs? There is no need to cry, Simone, because CloClo is right here, with our children. He sips on the cocktail I made him and comments on how refreshing it is and then he tells me I look very fetching today. I go to the record player and I put on one of his records. First we listen to 'Le téléphone pleure' and then 'J'attendrai.' We love to listen to his records together. And the children dance for us! Oh, it is so adorable to see them dance.

"I am the luckiest girl in the world! You must come and visit us this summer!"

THE BURDEN

While I slept, Nazis chased me up the staircase in the elementary school and I ran into a classroom, right up to the front, where the teacher would stand and teach, and I pulled down the big map of the world that the teacher would tap against with a pointer, and I hid behind it, and if you walked into the room it would be like there was a map with legs.

The Nazis shouldered their way into the classroom and started shooting, and soon the map was speckled with bullet holes. I felt myself falling.

I never remember my dreams, so this never happened. It didn't happen in real life and it didn't happen while I slept. It is not fact.

But since I don't remember my dreams, I guess it might have happened, after all. In my dreams. Which would mean, because I don't remember my dreams, that this would be a huge coincidence—that I dreamed about being chased in the school by Nazis and then, not remembering the dream, I made up a dream about being chased in the school by Nazis and it turned out to be the dream that I actually had.

I make sure I'm awake by poking a pencil into the palm of my hand and feeling whether it hurts me, which it does. I decide to say that I had a dream last week in which I am rolling up the side of a building, curled like a boll weevil, and I tumble into a window, and my mother and father and brother, all of whom are dead, are in the room I land in. They all say hi and they say they forgive me for not saying the things I should have said to them, and, in my brother's case, not trying hard enough to understand him, and they say I shouldn't feel guilty about anything and that they're okay with me.

Then I wait and see if my guilt disappears, as it would have if I really had that dream last week, and the dream was so real I thought it was a kind of visitation by the dead in my family. Them all coming back to forgive me and take the burden from me that rests on my shoulders and wrecks my posture.

And then I am filling a duffel bag with blank videotapes and hoping I can finish before the police arrive. And then I am at the breakfast table and my mother is serving me toast and she has forgotten that she died. And then a siren is going off and the sky turns red and I am cupping a dead baby bird in my hand.

I drift off while lying on the grass in a park and non-dead birds come lift me, holding my sleeves and pant legs in their beaks, and I rise, past telephone wires, past treetops, and into the clouds. I am light. I feel free of guilt. Why did I feel guilty?

I hope that when I wake, I will remember this.

WHAT IS THE SOUND OF SMOKE?

You could have had the courtesy to say, "I'm sorry to hear she's unwell." That was the minimum you might have offered. You could have added, "I hope she feels better soon." Or even, "I hope she's not in pain."

I have often wondered why you found that so difficult. Or did it simply not occur to you? Is it that the business of art is more important than the health of one person you've never met?

The last time we spoke on the phone, I heard you make that noise. A steady intake of breath. *Hffffff.* Of course, you told me long ago you had quit smoking—*hffffff*—but whenever we're on the phone, I hear that sucking in of smoke. I actually don't care whether or not you smoke. But why did you go to the trouble of lying to me about quitting? What does it matter what I think? Now that *hffffff* irritates me whenever I hear it. It makes me grit my teeth. Much more of that gritting and, says my dentist, Rick Cameron, I'm going to have to get those chompers capped. It'll cost about four thousand dollars. You think I've got that kind of money?

But look, a guy walked up to me, carrying a cardboard box. There was no writing on it, and the top flaps were folded in, overlapping. I was standing at the bus stop. We have only two buses here—Bus No. 1 and Bus No. 2. They both stop at my stop, so I have to be careful which bus I'm boarding. One goes to the mall, and the other goes way the hell out to the pallet factory or the soda-cracker factory or whatever that factory out there on the edge of town is. I'm not sure, you're asking the wrong person, but they make something square and tasteless.

The guy put the box down right in front of me. He said, "Want to buy a stuffed monkey?"

I didn't know whether he meant a real stuffed monkey or a plush toy monkey with a little manufacturer's label sticking out from one of its feet. The label would say what the monkey was made of plus offer laundering instructions. With a real stuffed monkey, there would be no label, no laundering instructions.

"Do you mean a real one?" I asked.

"As opposed to a *picture* of one?" he asked.

"As opposed to a toy one," I said.

The guy bent over and picked up the box again. He had nicotine stains on his fingers, they were unmistakable. "You're crazy," he said, and he walked away. I noticed a little fabric flap sticking out from his right elbow. I wondered if it was a label that said what he was made of and also offered laundering instructions.

It was around that time that climate change happened. There were tornados and tsunamis and the hottest day in six decades. You walked home from the store with a fresh egg and by the time you got to your front porch it was hard-boiled and perched in a little cup.

Climate change was all because of things that humans did, like drive cars and manufacture Barbie dolls and incinerate garbage and bomb villages in developing countries. The results of all those activities, necessary for the continuation of capitalism, a system that got invented that guarantees personal liberties, was that the weather was going fucking crazy.

The President of the United States said, "Fucking crazy weather is a small price to pay for liberty." The next day at a grocery store he refused a paper bag and asked instead for his purchases to be triple-bagged in plastic. "They will not blackmail us into giving up our freedom," he said. "We will not let them win."

Truth was, I didn't want either kind of monkey. The guy was right to walk away. *Hffffff*.

It was pouring rain outside—a monsoon practically, and totally out of character for this season in this tiny town by the lake—and she was lying on the sofa sleeping under three blankets. She'd been sleeping the whole day. Almost the whole day anyway. Her face was relaxed and serene. The air conditioner was on and the cat was sleeping on the windowsill. He wanted to go out but we were scared he'd get hit by a car.

So I said she wasn't well, that she hadn't been for several months, and you gave me a deadline. You didn't say, "Why don't you take till [whatever day], and I hope she's feeling better soon." Instead, you were all business.

You might've said, "Oh shit, take as long as you need—her health is the most important thing." It'd still be only one sentence—I mean, if it was a matter of you being very busy when you responded. Unless you think I'm cheating with that em dash: claiming only one sentence when I'm actually using two.

For example, how do you feel about:

We've never had so much rain—this kind of torrential downpour is unprecedented.

The president holds freedom sacred—he triple-bags his groceries in plastic.

The man put the box right in front of me—he was selling a stuffed monkey.

The manufacturer's tag contains lots of information—it even tells you how to launder the thing.

Sorry I don't have it ready yet—my girlfriend's been under the weather the last few months and I've been preoccupied.

Do you think that I snuck a third sentence in with that last example, by using an "and" in addition to an em dash?

But look, if you weren't fussy about the number of sentences, you could even have added: "Let me know if there's anything I can do." That one has extra value. On the one hand, it offers great comfort, but on the other, it's unlikely—*hfffff*—you'll be asked to do anything.

Do you feel like going for a swim at the North Pole? I just found out it's melted. Not many people know yet, so it won't be too crowded. Best to go before word gets out, and then everyone and their mother will be there. I don't have anything against all-inclusive resorts, but imagine what it would be like to be in one of those paradises before the little hotel rooms are built and the buses are pulling in every twelve hours and guys are trying to sell you stuffed monkeys whenever you turn a corner. It'd be just you and the splendours of planet earth.

The cat is sleeping on the windowsill. Lately that's his favourite spot. We haven't let him out in over a year, so outside is sort of like a TV show for him. At least, that's what we hope. When he wants his head scratched, right between the ears, he tilts his nose up just slightly, and his tongue pokes out just past his teeth, cupped as if asking for alms.

THE DEAD
FROG
OF LOVE

The squashed frog on the tarmac was calling my name. I could hear it distinctly. No one else seemed to notice. They just streamed by, wiping their brows against the sudden heat, eager to begin building their collection of I Heart Managua souvenirs. I knelt.

The side of the frog was split open, and red and yellow blobby things were poking out of it. I tugged my baseball cap down over my brow to block out the glare of the sun, which hovered directly above. This wasn't one of those dried-up frogs you find tangled into a dust bunny in the corner of your Grade 3 classroom. This was a freshly dead creature, who just hours or even minutes ago was hopping along thinking about whatever it is frogs think about.

A couple of bubbles surged out from the slit in its side, and I realized the little guy had begun to actually cook. This was where the country had gotten its motto: Nicaragua: Where You Can Broil Dead Animals on the Sidewalk, Especially in July. I reached into my shirt pocket and took out a pack of cigarettes. I opened it, emptied the cigarettes into my other shirt pocket, and gently scooped the frog into the cigarette pack. I looked up and saw a uniformed soldier watching me from near the terminal door. She was squinting and grinning. I was a crazy gringo.

When I arrived at my hotel, Casa Leonel Rugama, a message was waiting for me from the Oficina del Turismo de Nicaragua. I knew no Spanish, as I had never been farther than Sudbury before, but I did recognize my name among all the foreign words, and I could figure out "Oficina" and "Turismo." Well, they weren't really foreign words, because I was in the country of these words. I was what was foreign. I wondered how you said "frog" in Spanish, because I wondered if this was about the frog in the cigarette packet in my shirt pocket. Were you allowed to pick up dead frogs in this country?

No, I was sure that wasn't it. If it had been, the letter would have come from the Oficina del Policismo instead of the Oficinia del Turismo. I thought about that soldier who had been watching me. I wondered if I was in love with her. I had been to Sudbury six times and had never fallen in love. But in Managua I had fallen in love within minutes of arriving. I had found a dead frog and love. I pulled my tiny Spanish-English dictionary out of my back pants pocket and flipped through it. I found *muerto*, *rana*, and *querer*.

My hotel room was about two metres by four metres. The bed was a thin mattress on a plank of wood. A fan sat on a narrow wooden ledge nailed to the wall. I turned it on and put my face into the breeze. I tried to remember why I'd come to Nicaragua. A small lizard clung to the wall beside my bed and looked me right in the eyes.

The bar was tiny and had a thatched roof and no walls. Where I was from, in the small town of Cobourg, on Lake Ontario, our bars had walls. The same with Sudbury. Four walls to every bar. If one travelled to find something different, then this was definitely travelling. I couldn't wait to tell people back home what I had seen. Also, instead of tables in this bar, there were large, overturned spools that had been used for, I assumed, telephone wire. These were surrounded by roughly made wooden stools. On the stools sat a dozen or so young Nicaraguans. I stood facing the non-existent wall in the front of the bar. I was flanked by a man with a regular-size guitar and a man with a very tiny guitar. I looked to them, one at a time, and nodded, and they nodded back, one at a time.

A woman wearing a white cotton shirt and blue jeans stepped in front of us and said something in Spanish. The audience cheered. The two guitarists struck some chords, then paused. All eyes were on me. I thought for a moment, holding back the panic, then drew the cigarette pack out of my shirt. I lifted the lid and drew the frog out a bit, so that it looked like it was peeking out of the box. I turned it toward the audience.

Then the guitarists began to play. The chords from the big guitar were deep, like the voice of Lurch from *The Munsters*. The chords from the tiny guitar were jingly, like the rain that had fallen on the metal roof of my hotel room at Casa Leonel Rugama the night before. Below my nose was a mouth, and this I then opened.

> *The rana may be muerte*
> *but still he is in querer*
> *with the lady soldier*
> *who was standing by the door*
> *of the terminal*
> *at Agosto Sandino Internacionalismo!*
>
> *Sing, Nicaragua, sing!*
> *The rana may be muerte*
> *but still he is in querer!*

The guitarists struck their final chords. I had done it. I had performed with a band in Managua, Nicaragua. I couldn't remember if that is what I had come to do, or even how I had found myself at this bar, but the audience went crazy. By which I mean, they shook their heads in disbelief and began laughing. One of them yelled, "Más cerveza!" which I took to mean "Service for everybody," because the waiters seemed so slow to look after the guests.

As I walked the dark and warm streets of Managua after my success at the bar with no walls, I fell into an open sewer. I remembered a trick I'd learned from a television show back home. I again drew the cigarette box from my pocket, then flung it up onto the road. It was only a matter of time before the dead frog of love attracted the attention of the beautiful soldier, and my life would change.

ACKNOWLEDGEMENTS

Earlier versions of some of these stories have appeared in print and online. Thank you to the editors of these publications.

"The Elements of the Short Story" appeared in *subTerrain*.

"The Burden" appeared online at *BoulderPavement*.

"Don't Touch People's Heads" appeared in *Event*.

"I Am Claude François and You Are a Bathtub" appeared in *Exile Literary Quarterly*.

"Housing," "Remember the Story," "Skunk Problem at the Food Booth," and "Strength and Confidence" appeared in *Taddle Creek*.

"Lee Marvin, at Your Service" appeared in *This Magazine*.

"The Sound of Smoke" appeared in the anthology *The Sound of Smoke* (Teksteditions, 2014).

"Evidence" appeared in *Rampike*.

"Things Fell on Him" appeared in *In/Words*.

"The Dead Frog of Love" appeared online in *EPIZOOTICS!* Thanks to Sarah Steinberg for the motivation to write it.

Thanks to Jaime Forsythe, Elyse Friedman, and Laurie Siblock for their smart feedback on various of these stories. The potato in "La Papa" was discovered in the microwave by Christine Miscione.

Gratitude to the Anvil crew: Brian Kaufman, Karen Green, and Jessica Key. And to Clint Hutzulak at rayola.com for another dream cover. Thanks to Laurie Siblock for her eagle-eyed proofread.

And thank you to the people of Ontario for generous support through the Ontario Arts Council and the people of Canada for generous support through the Canada Council for the Arts.

ABOUT THE AUTHOR

Stuart Ross is a writer, editor, writing teacher, and small press activist living in Cobourg, Ontario. The recipient of the 2019 Harbourfront Festival Prize, the 2017 Canadian Jewish Literary Award for Poetry, and the 2010 Relit Prize for Short Fiction, among others, Stuart is the author of over twenty books of poetry, fiction, memoir, and essays, most recently *The Book of Grief and Hamburgers* and *70 Kippers: The Dagmar Poems* (with Michael Dennis). Stuart has taught workshops across the country and was Writer-in-Residence at Queen's University and the University of Ottawa. He has given hundreds of readings of his fiction, poetry, creative nonfiction, and sound poetry in Canada, the US, the UK, Slovenia, Nicaragua, and Chile. His work has been translated into French, Nynorsk, Slovene, Russian, Spanish, and Estonian. Stuart occasionally blogs at bloggamooga.blogspot.ca.